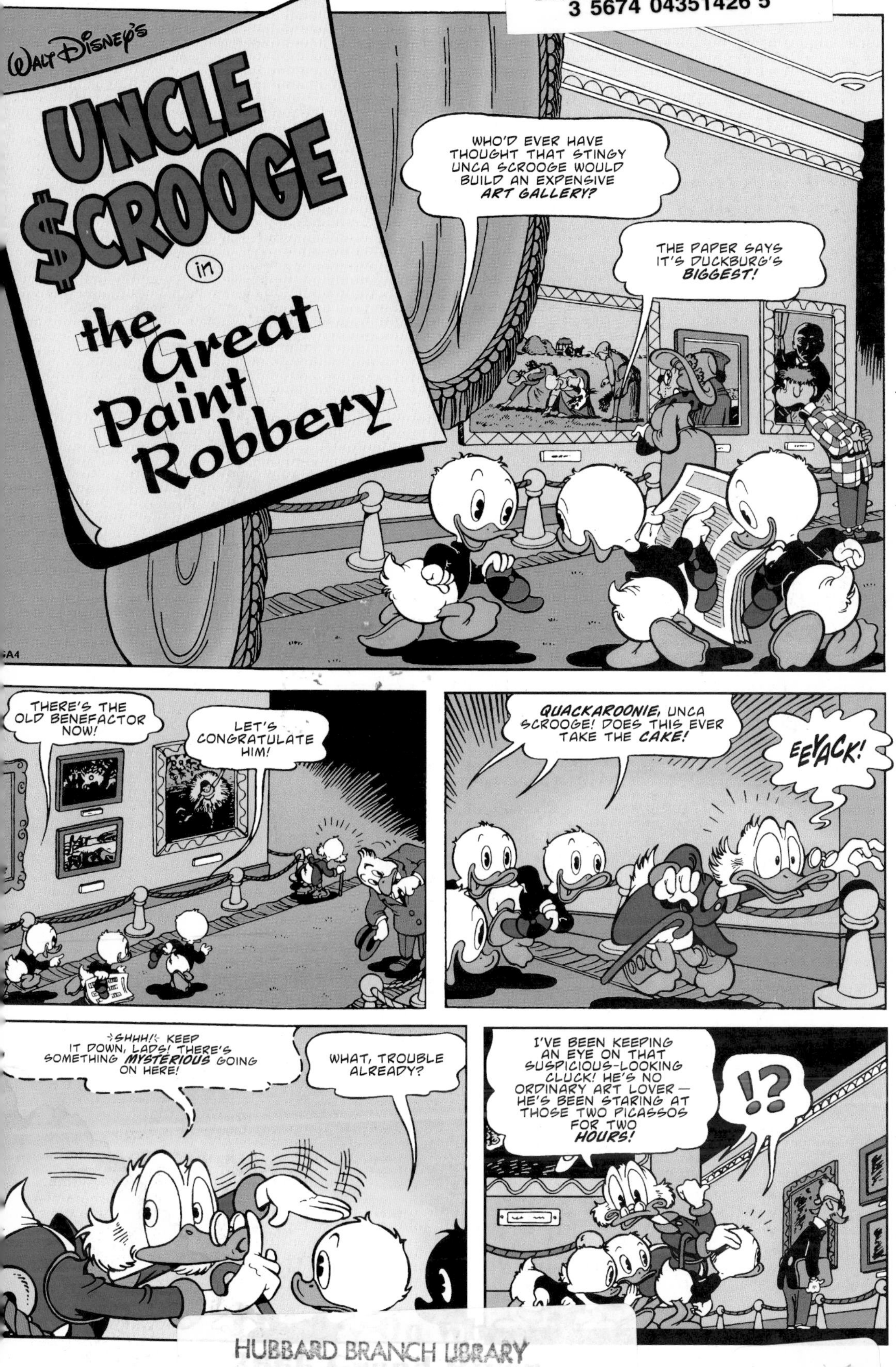
WALT DISNEY'S
UNCLE $CROOGE
in
the Great Paint Robbery
WHO'D EVER HAVE THOUGHT THAT STINGY UNCA SCROOGE WOULD BUILD AN EXPENSIVE ART GALLERY?
THE PAPER SAYS IT'S DUCKBURG'S BIGGEST!
THERE'S THE OLD BENEFACTOR NOW!
LET'S CONGRATULATE HIM!
QUACKAROONIE, UNCA SCROOGE! DOES THIS EVER TAKE THE CAKE!
EEYACK!
SHHH! KEEP IT DOWN, LADS! THERE'S SOMETHING MYSTERIOUS GOING ON HERE!
WHAT, TROUBLE ALREADY?
I'VE BEEN KEEPING AN EYE ON THAT SUSPICIOUS-LOOKING CLUCK! HE'S NO ORDINARY ART LOVER— HE'S BEEN STARING AT THOSE TWO PICASSOS FOR TWO HOURS!
!?

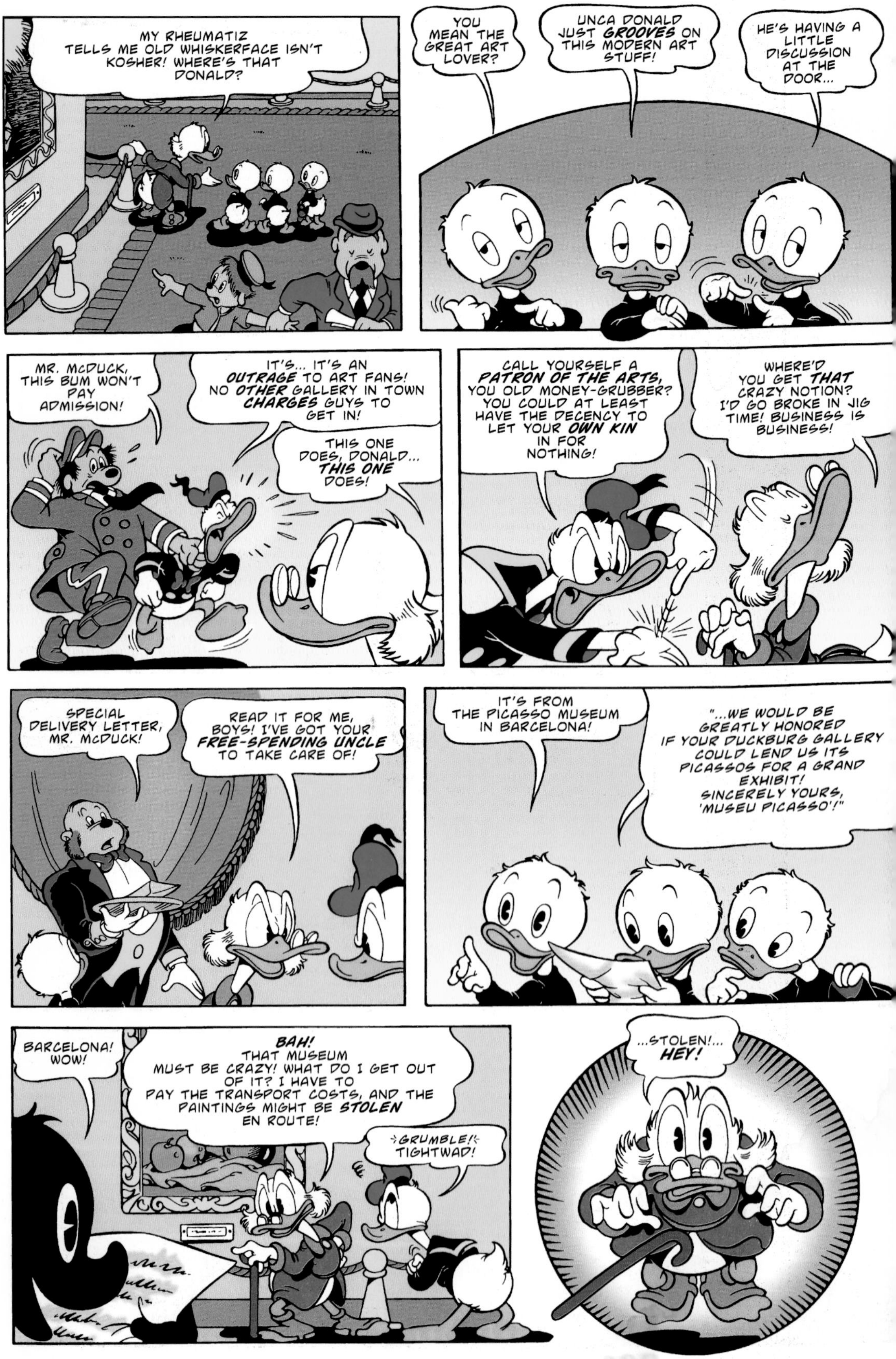
MY RHEUMATIZ TELLS ME OLD WHISKERFACE ISN'T KOSHER! WHERE'S THAT DONALD?
YOU MEAN THE GREAT ART LOVER?
UNCA DONALD JUST GROOVES ON THIS MODERN ART STUFF!
HE'S HAVING A LITTLE DISCUSSION AT THE DOOR...
MR. McDUCK, THIS BUM WON'T PAY ADMISSION!
IT'S... IT'S AN OUTRAGE TO ART FANS! NO OTHER GALLERY IN TOWN CHARGES GUYS TO GET IN!
THIS ONE DOES, DONALD... THIS ONE DOES!
CALL YOURSELF A PATRON OF THE ARTS, YOU OLD MONEY-GRUBBER? YOU COULD AT LEAST HAVE THE DECENCY TO LET YOUR OWN KIN IN FOR NOTHING!
WHERE'D YOU GET THAT CRAZY NOTION? I'D GO BROKE IN JIG TIME! BUSINESS IS BUSINESS!
SPECIAL DELIVERY LETTER, MR. McDUCK!
READ IT FOR ME, BOYS! I'VE GOT YOUR FREE-SPENDING UNCLE TO TAKE CARE OF!
IT'S FROM THE PICASSO MUSEUM IN BARCELONA!
"...WE WOULD BE GREATLY HONORED IF YOUR DUCKBURG GALLERY COULD LEND US ITS PICASSOS FOR A GRAND EXHIBIT! SINCERELY YOURS, 'MUSEU PICASSO'!"
BARCELONA! WOW!
BAH! THAT MUSEUM MUST BE CRAZY! WHAT DO I GET OUT OF IT? I HAVE TO PAY THE TRANSPORT COSTS, AND THE PAINTINGS MIGHT BE STOLEN EN ROUTE!
GRUMBLE! TIGHTWAD!
...STOLEN!... HEY!

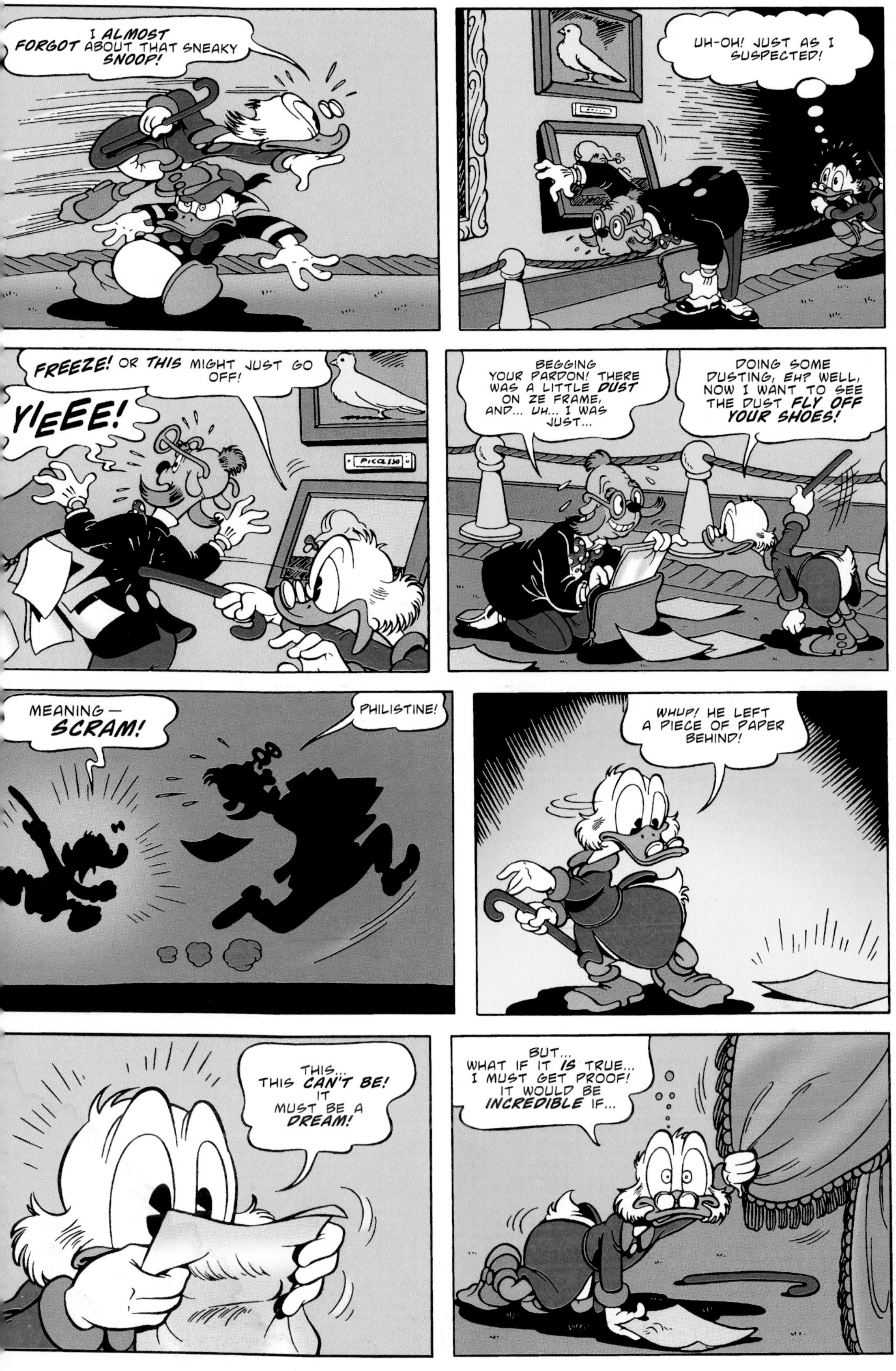
I ALMOST FORGOT ABOUT THAT SNEAKY SNOOP!
UH-OH! JUST AS I SUSPECTED!
FREEZE! OR THIS MIGHT JUST GO OFF!
Y'EEEE!
PICASSO
BEGGING YOUR PARDON! THERE WAS A LITTLE DUST ON ZE FRAME, AND... UH... I WAS JUST...
DOING SOME DUSTING, EH? WELL, NOW I WANT TO SEE THE DUST FLY OFF YOUR SHOES!
MEANING— SCRAM!
PHILISTINE!
WHUP! HE LEFT A PIECE OF PAPER BEHIND!
THIS... THIS CAN'T BE! IT MUST BE A DREAM!
BUT... WHAT IF IT IS TRUE... I MUST GET PROOF! IT WOULD BE INCREDIBLE IF...

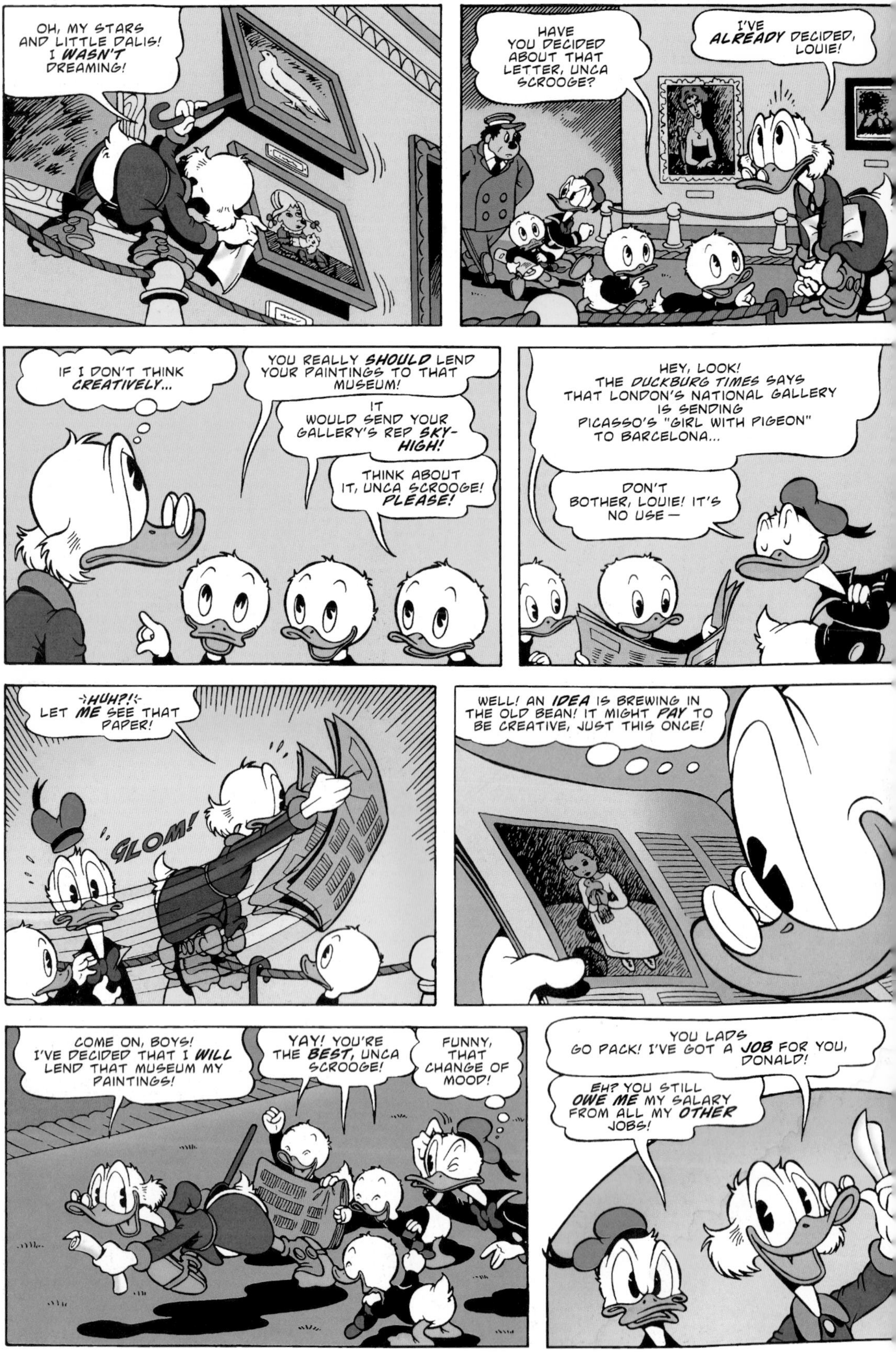

OH, MY STARS AND LITTLE DALIS! I WASN'T DREAMING!
HAVE YOU DECIDED ABOUT THAT LETTER, UNCA SCROOGE?
I'VE ALREADY DECIDED, LOUIE!
IF I DON'T THINK CREATIVELY...
YOU REALLY SHOULD LEND YOUR PAINTINGS TO THAT MUSEUM!
IT WOULD SEND YOUR GALLERY'S REP SKY-HIGH!
THINK ABOUT IT, UNCA SCROOGE! PLEASE!
HEY, LOOK! THE DUCKBURG TIMES SAYS THAT LONDON'S NATIONAL GALLERY IS SENDING PICASSO'S "GIRL WITH PIGEON" TO BARCELONA...
DON'T BOTHER, LOUIE! IT'S NO USE —
HUH?! LET ME SEE THAT PAPER!
GLOM!
WELL! AN IDEA IS BREWING IN THE OLD BEAN! IT MIGHT PAY TO BE CREATIVE, JUST THIS ONCE!
COME ON, BOYS! I'VE DECIDED THAT I WILL LEND THAT MUSEUM MY PAINTINGS!
YAY! YOU'RE THE BEST, UNCA SCROOGE!
FUNNY, THAT CHANGE OF MOOD!
YOU LADS GO PACK! I'VE GOT A JOB FOR YOU, DONALD!
EH? YOU STILL OWE ME MY SALARY FROM ALL MY OTHER JOBS!

35674043514265

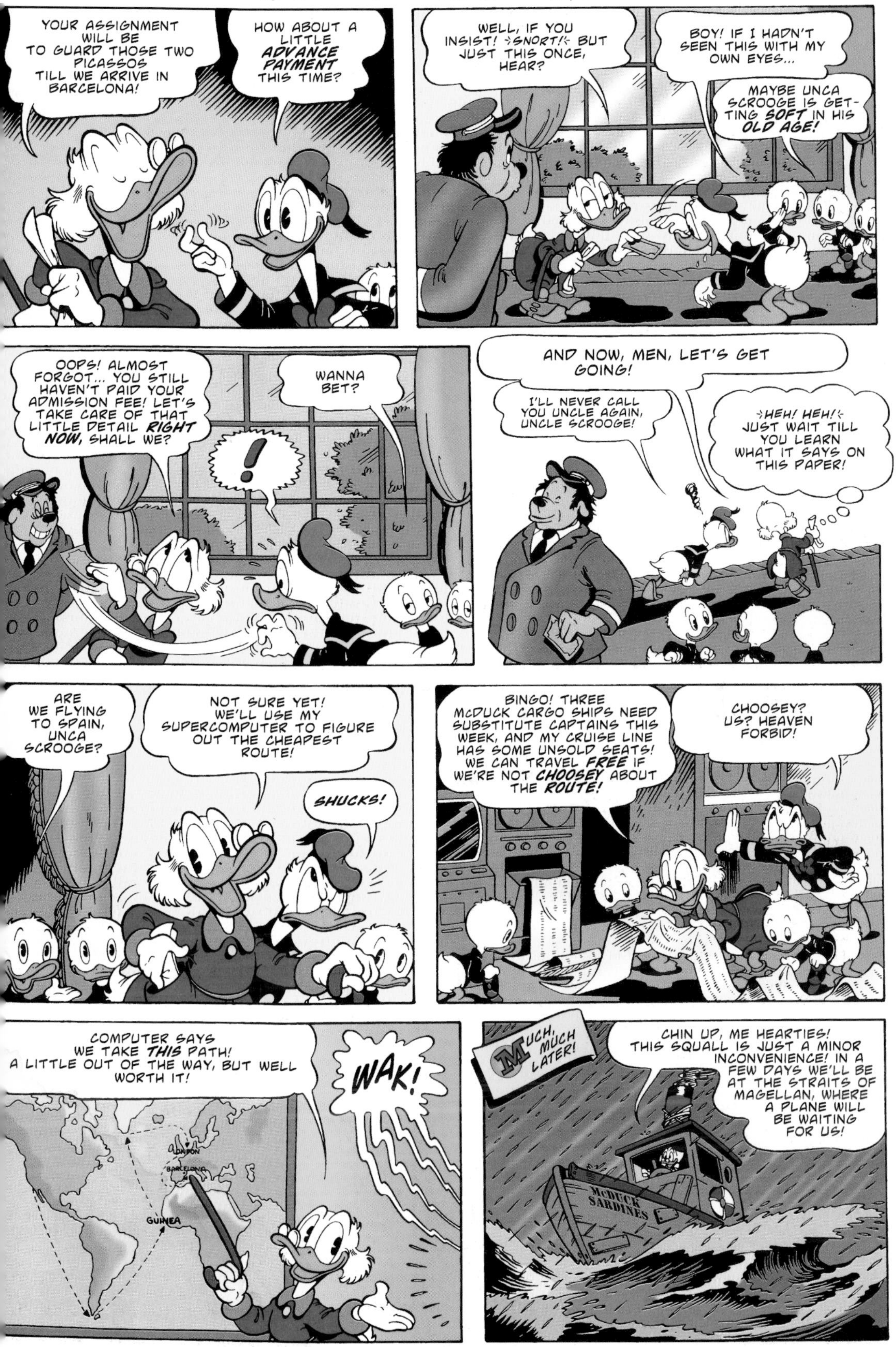

YOUR ASSIGNMENT WILL BE TO GUARD THOSE TWO PICASSOS TILL WE ARRIVE IN BARCELONA!
HOW ABOUT A LITTLE ADVANCE PAYMENT THIS TIME?
WELL, IF YOU INSIST! SNORT! BUT JUST THIS ONCE, HEAR?
BOY! IF I HADN'T SEEN THIS WITH MY OWN EYES...
MAYBE UNCA SCROOGE IS GETTING SOFT IN HIS OLD AGE!
OOPS! ALMOST FORGOT... YOU STILL HAVEN'T PAID YOUR ADMISSION FEE! LET'S TAKE CARE OF THAT LITTLE DETAIL RIGHT NOW, SHALL WE?
WANNA BET?
!
AND NOW, MEN, LET'S GET GOING!
I'LL NEVER CALL YOU UNCLE AGAIN, UNCLE SCROOGE!
HEH! HEH! JUST WAIT TILL YOU LEARN WHAT IT SAYS ON THIS PAPER!
ARE WE FLYING TO SPAIN, UNCA SCROOGE?
NOT SURE YET! WE'LL USE MY SUPERCOMPUTER TO FIGURE OUT THE CHEAPEST ROUTE!
SHUCKS!
BINGO! THREE McDUCK CARGO SHIPS NEED SUBSTITUTE CAPTAINS THIS WEEK, AND MY CRUISE LINE HAS SOME UNSOLD SEATS! WE CAN TRAVEL FREE IF WE'RE NOT CHOOSEY ABOUT THE ROUTE!
CHOOSEY? US? HEAVEN FORBID!
COMPUTER SAYS WE TAKE THIS PATH! A LITTLE OUT OF THE WAY, BUT WELL WORTH IT!
LONDON
BARCELONA
GUINEA
WAK!
MUCH, MUCH LATER!
CHIN UP, ME HEARTIES! THIS SQUALL IS JUST A MINOR INCONVENIENCE! IN A FEW DAYS WE'LL BE AT THE STRAITS OF MAGELLAN, WHERE A PLANE WILL BE WAITING FOR US!
McDUCK SARDINES

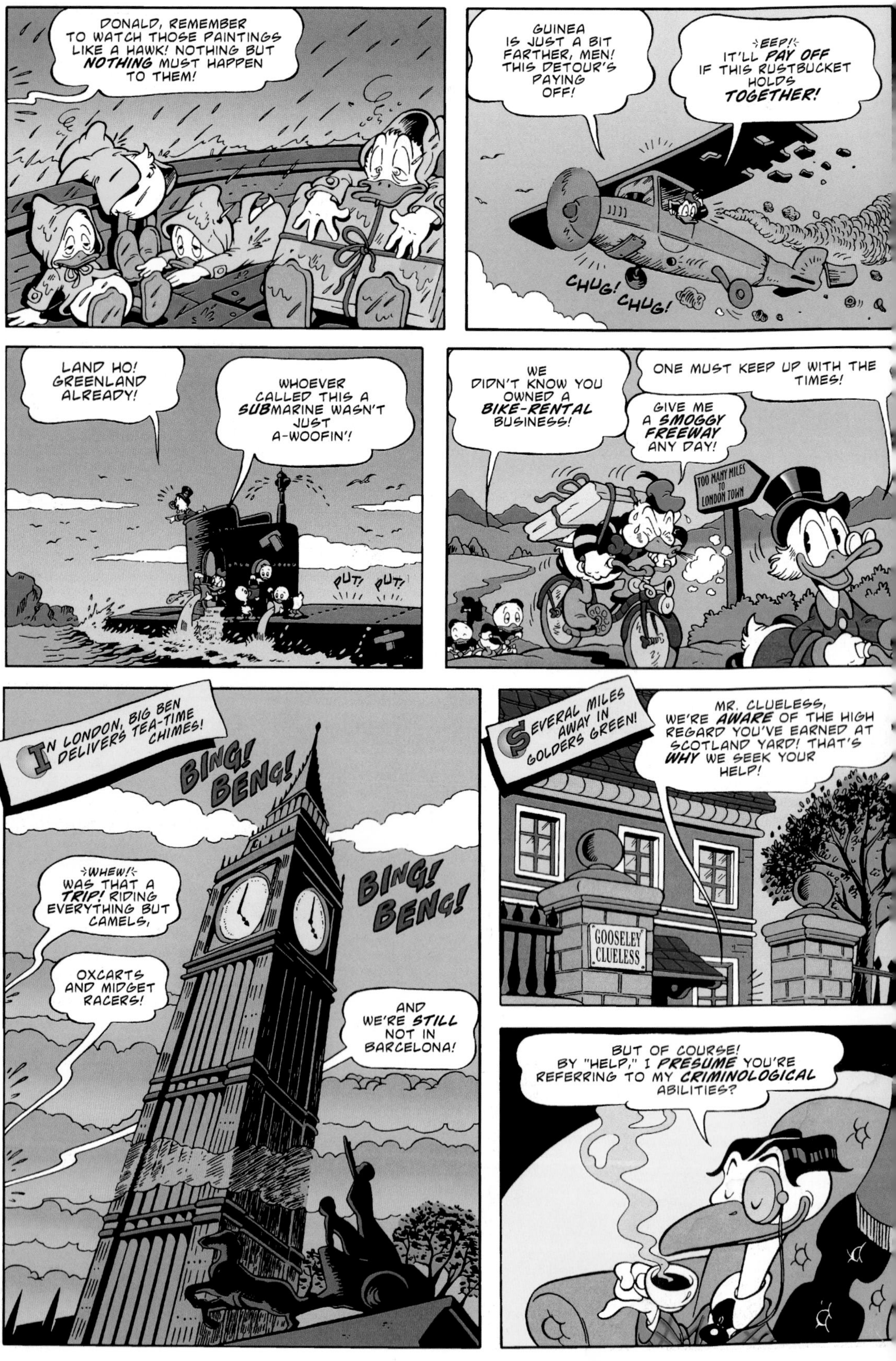
DONALD, REMEMBER TO WATCH THOSE PAINTINGS LIKE A HAWK! NOTHING BUT NOTHING MUST HAPPEN TO THEM!
GUINEA IS JUST A BIT FARTHER, MEN! THIS DETOUR'S PAYING OFF!
EEP! IT'LL PAY OFF IF THIS RUSTBUCKET HOLDS TOGETHER!
CHUG! CHUG!
LAND HO! GREENLAND ALREADY!
WHOEVER CALLED THIS A SUBMARINE WASN'T JUST A-WOOFIN'!
PUT! PUT!
WE DIDN'T KNOW YOU OWNED A BIKE-RENTAL BUSINESS!
ONE MUST KEEP UP WITH THE TIMES!
GIVE ME A SMOGGY FREEWAY ANY DAY!
TOO MANY MILES TO LONDON TOWN
IN LONDON, BIG BEN DELIVERS TEA-TIME CHIMES!
BING! BENG!
BING! BENG!
WHEW! WAS THAT A TRIP! RIDING EVERYTHING BUT CAMELS,
OXCARTS AND MIDGET RACERS!
AND WE'RE STILL NOT IN BARCELONA!
SEVERAL MILES AWAY IN GOLDERS GREEN!
MR. CLUELESS, WE'RE AWARE OF THE HIGH REGARD YOU'VE EARNED AT SCOTLAND YARD! THAT'S WHY WE SEEK YOUR HELP!
GOOSELEY CLUELESS
BUT OF COURSE! BY "HELP," I PRESUME YOU'RE REFERRING TO MY CRIMINOLOGICAL ABILITIES?

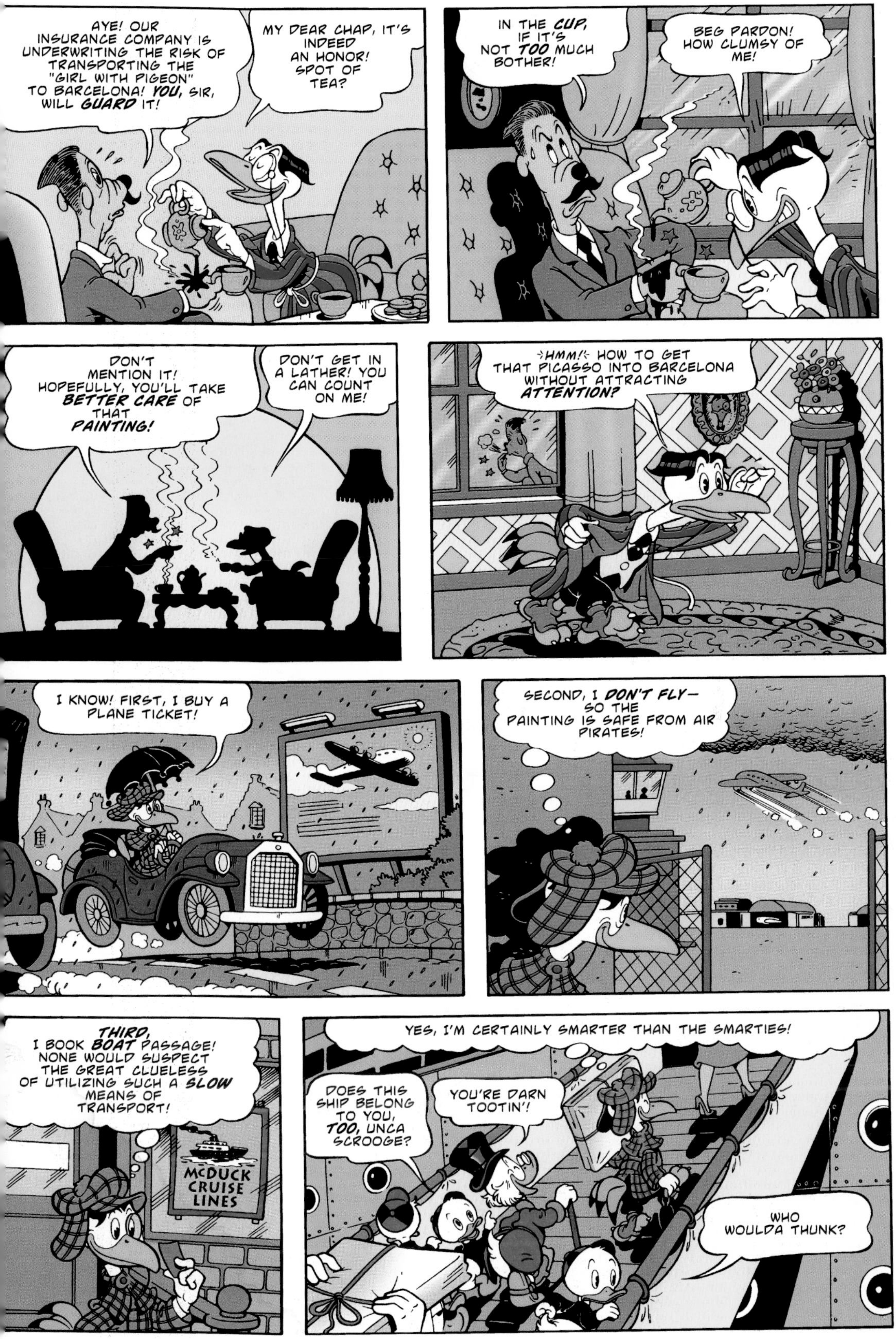
AYE! OUR INSURANCE COMPANY IS UNDERWRITING THE RISK OF TRANSPORTING THE "GIRL WITH PIGEON" TO BARCELONA! YOU, SIR, WILL GUARD IT!
MY DEAR CHAP, IT'S INDEED AN HONOR! SPOT OF TEA?
IN THE CUP, IF IT'S NOT TOO MUCH BOTHER!
BEG PARDON! HOW CLUMSY OF ME!
DON'T MENTION IT! HOPEFULLY, YOU'LL TAKE BETTER CARE OF THAT PAINTING!
DON'T GET IN A LATHER! YOU CAN COUNT ON ME!
HMM! HOW TO GET THAT PICASSO INTO BARCELONA WITHOUT ATTRACTING ATTENTION?
I KNOW! FIRST, I BUY A PLANE TICKET!
SECOND, I DON'T FLY— SO THE PAINTING IS SAFE FROM AIR PIRATES!
THIRD, I BOOK BOAT PASSAGE! NONE WOULD SUSPECT THE GREAT CLUELESS OF UTILIZING SUCH A SLOW MEANS OF TRANSPORT!
McDUCK CRUISE LINES
YES, I'M CERTAINLY SMARTER THAN THE SMARTIES!
DOES THIS SHIP BELONG TO YOU, TOO, UNCA SCROOGE?
YOU'RE DARN TOOTIN'!
WHO WOULDA THUNK?

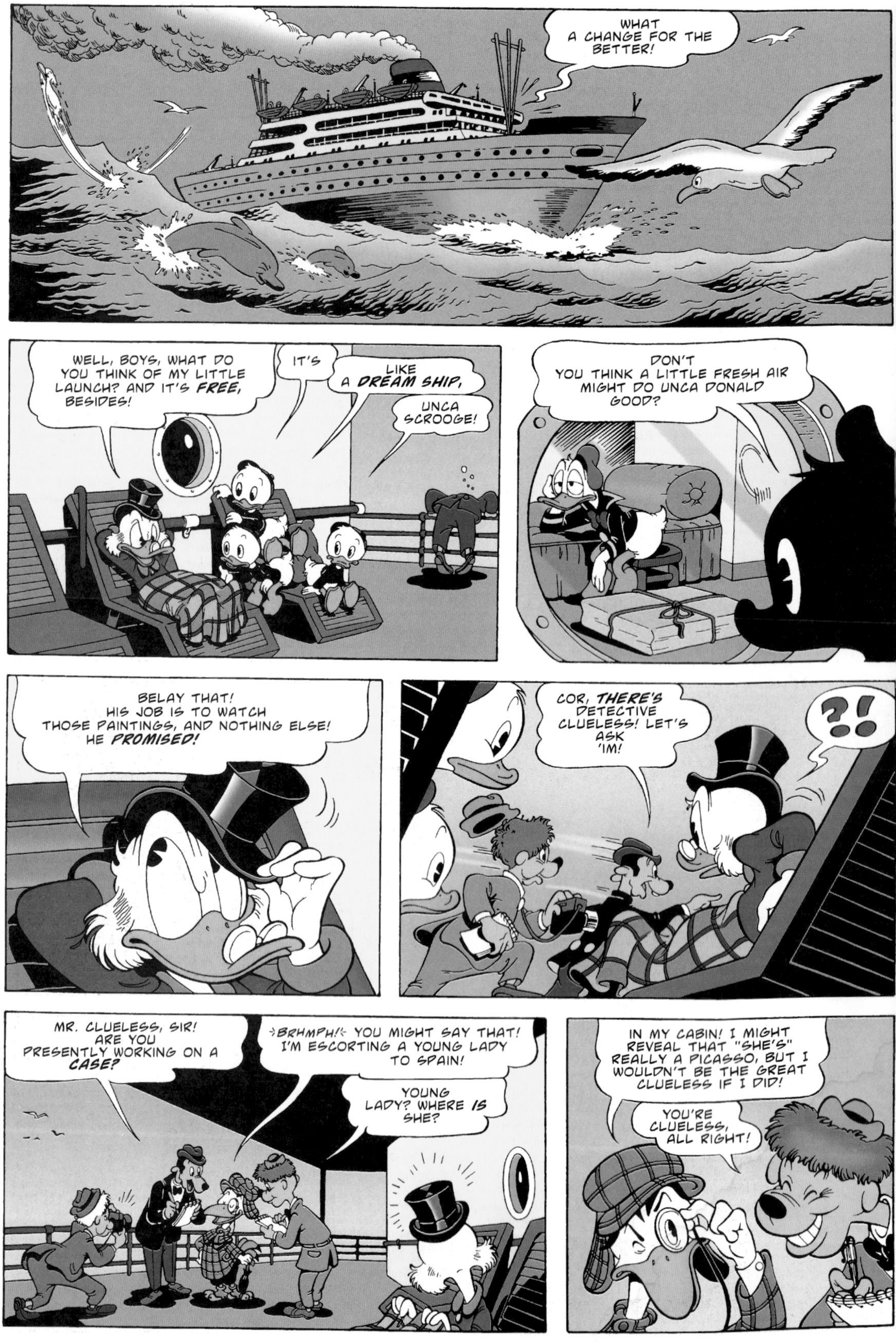
WHAT A CHANGE FOR THE BETTER!
WELL, BOYS, WHAT DO YOU THINK OF MY LITTLE LAUNCH? AND IT'S FREE, BESIDES!
IT'S
LIKE A DREAM SHIP,
UNCA SCROOGE!
DON'T YOU THINK A LITTLE FRESH AIR MIGHT DO UNCA DONALD GOOD?
BELAY THAT! HIS JOB IS TO WATCH THOSE PAINTINGS, AND NOTHING ELSE! HE PROMISED!
COR, THERE'S DETECTIVE CLUELESS! LET'S ASK 'IM!
?!
MR. CLUELESS, SIR! ARE YOU PRESENTLY WORKING ON A CASE?
BRHMPH! YOU MIGHT SAY THAT! I'M ESCORTING A YOUNG LADY TO SPAIN!
YOUNG LADY? WHERE IS SHE?
IN MY CABIN! I MIGHT REVEAL THAT "SHE'S" REALLY A PICASSO, BUT I WOULDN'T BE THE GREAT CLUELESS IF I DID!
YOU'RE CLUELESS, ALL RIGHT!

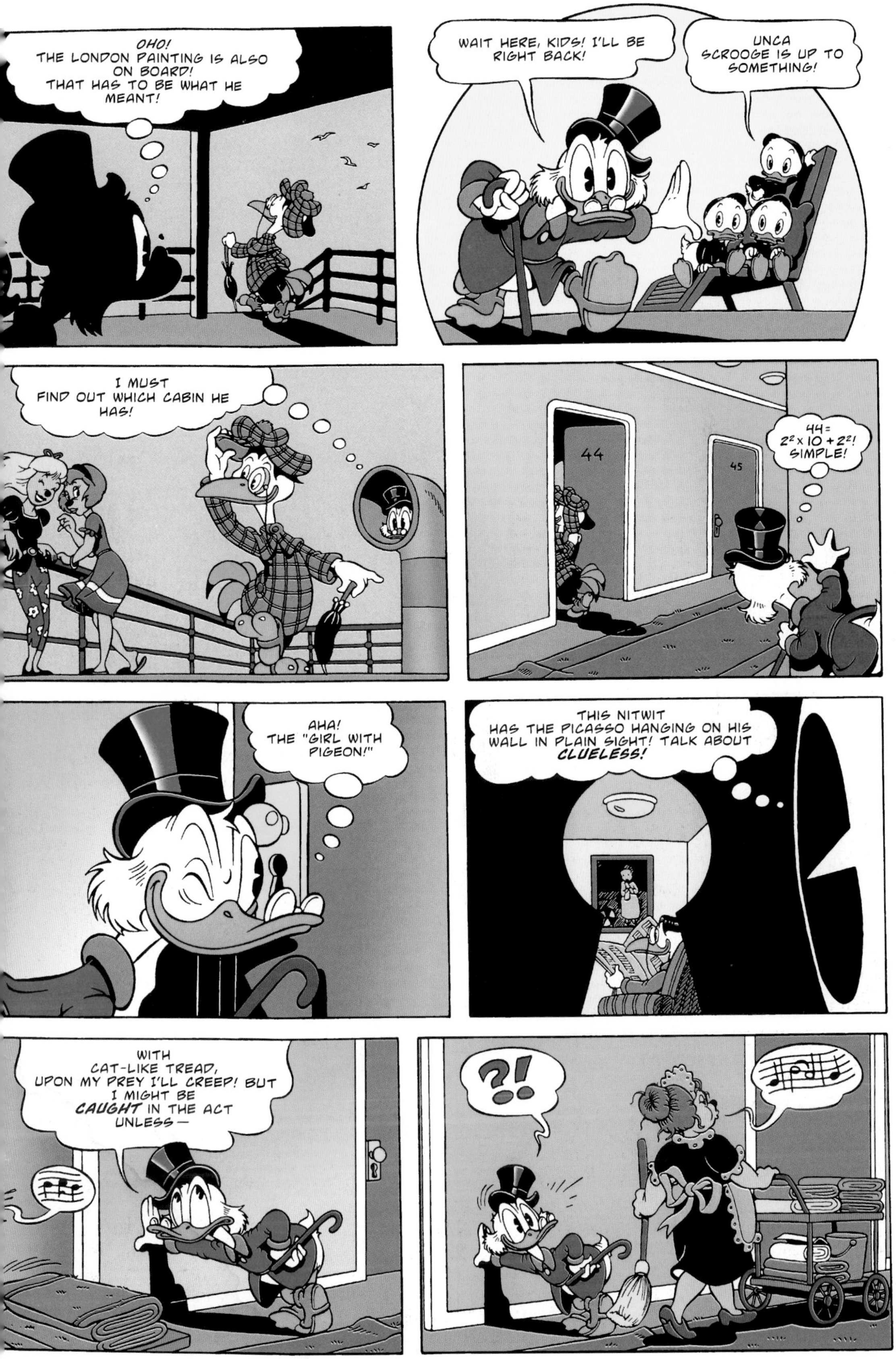
OHO! THE LONDON PAINTING IS ALSO ON BOARD! THAT HAS TO BE WHAT HE MEANT!
WAIT HERE, KIDS! I'LL BE RIGHT BACK!
UNCA SCROOGE IS UP TO SOMETHING!
I MUST FIND OUT WHICH CABIN HE HAS!
44
45
44= $2^2 \times 10 + 2^2$! SIMPLE!
AHA! THE "GIRL WITH PIGEON!"
THIS NITWIT HAS THE PICASSO HANGING ON HIS WALL IN PLAIN SIGHT! TALK ABOUT ***CLUELESS!***
WITH CAT-LIKE TREAD, UPON MY PREY I'LL CREEP! BUT I MIGHT BE ***CAUGHT*** IN THE ACT UNLESS—
?!

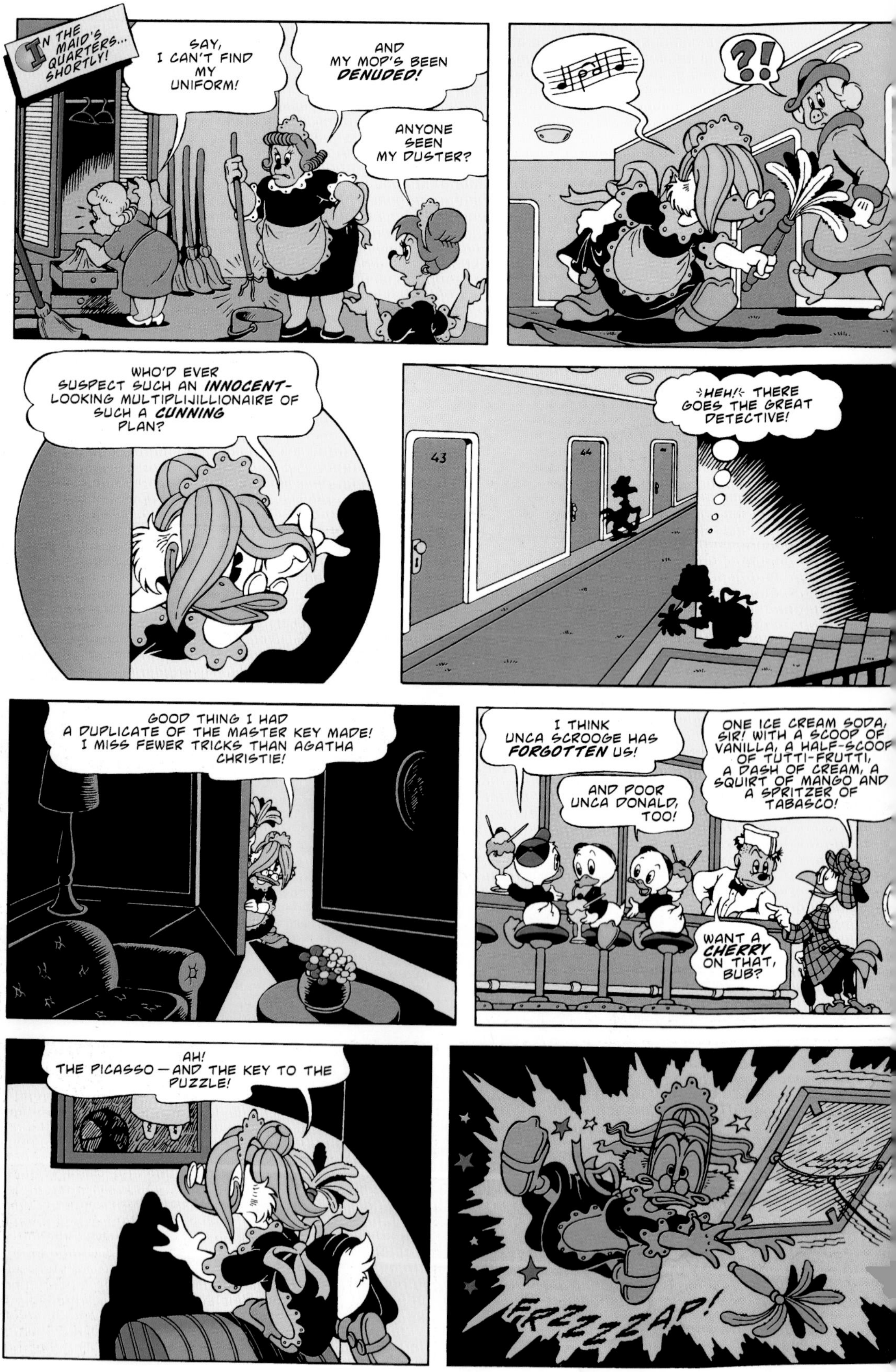
IN THE MAID'S QUARTERS... SHORTLY!
SAY, I CAN'T FIND MY UNIFORM!
AND MY MOP'S BEEN DENUDED!
ANYONE SEEN MY DUSTER?
?!
WHO'D EVER SUSPECT SUCH AN INNOCENT-LOOKING MULTIPLIJILLIONAIRE OF SUCH A CUNNING PLAN?
43
44
HEH! THERE GOES THE GREAT DETECTIVE!
GOOD THING I HAD A DUPLICATE OF THE MASTER KEY MADE! I MISS FEWER TRICKS THAN AGATHA CHRISTIE!
I THINK UNCA SCROOGE HAS FORGOTTEN US!
AND POOR UNCA DONALD, TOO!
ONE ICE CREAM SODA, SIR! WITH A SCOOP OF VANILLA, A HALF-SCOOP OF TUTTI-FRUTTI, A DASH OF CREAM, A SQUIRT OF MANGO AND A SPRITZER OF TABASCO!
WANT A CHERRY ON THAT, BUB?
AH! THE PICASSO — AND THE KEY TO THE PUZZLE!
FRZZZZZAP!

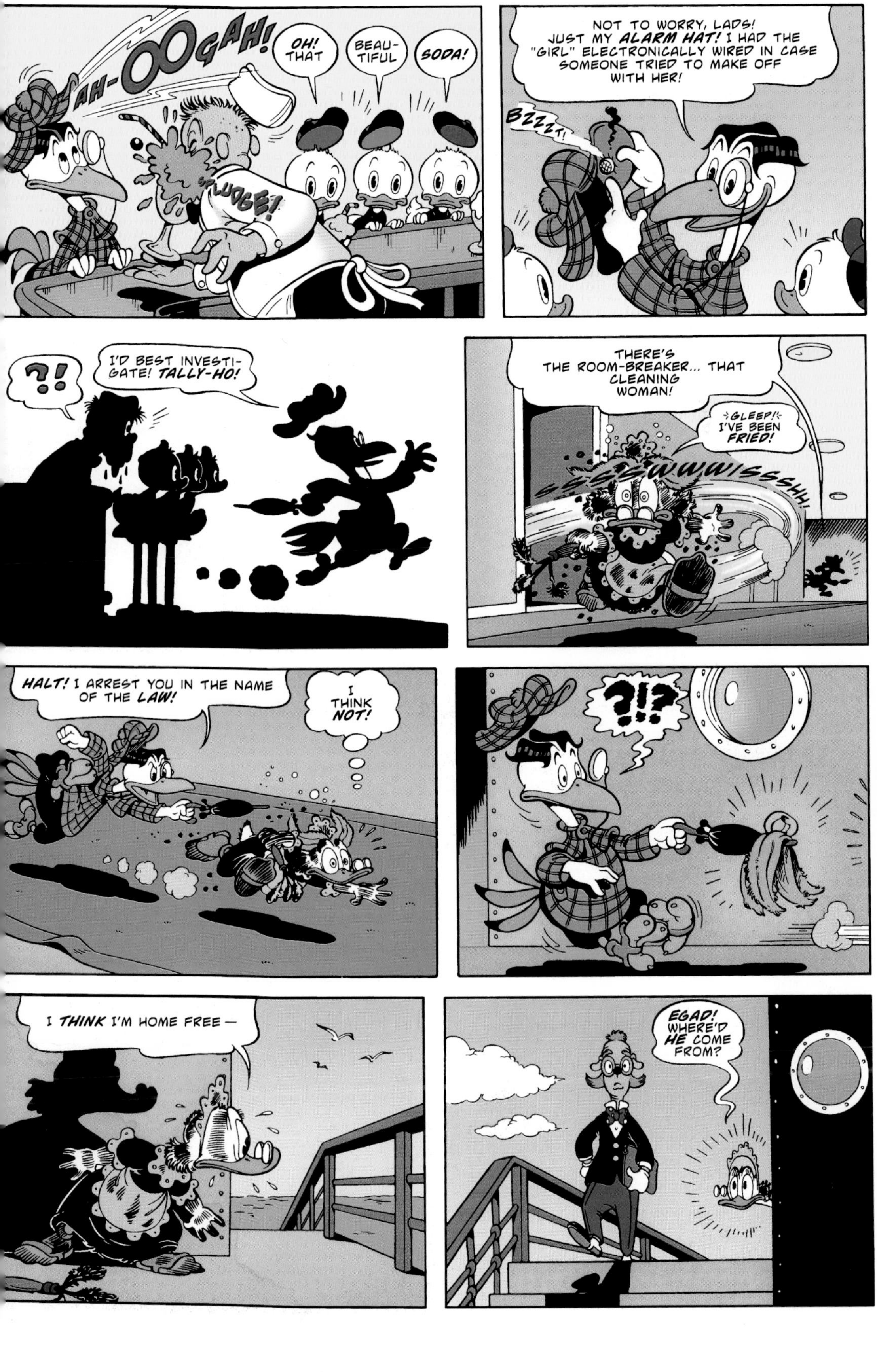
AH-OOGAH!
OH! THAT
BEAU-TIFUL
SODA!
NOT TO WORRY, LADS! JUST MY ALARM HAT! I HAD THE "GIRL" ELECTRONICALLY WIRED IN CASE SOMEONE TRIED TO MAKE OFF WITH HER!
BZZZZT!
?!
I'D BEST INVESTI-GATE! TALLY-HO!
THERE'S THE ROOM-BREAKER... THAT CLEANING WOMAN!
GLEEP! I'VE BEEN FRIED!
SSSSWWW!SSSHH!
HALT! I ARREST YOU IN THE NAME OF THE LAW!
I THINK NOT!
?!?
I THINK I'M HOME FREE —
EGAD! WHERE'D HE COME FROM?

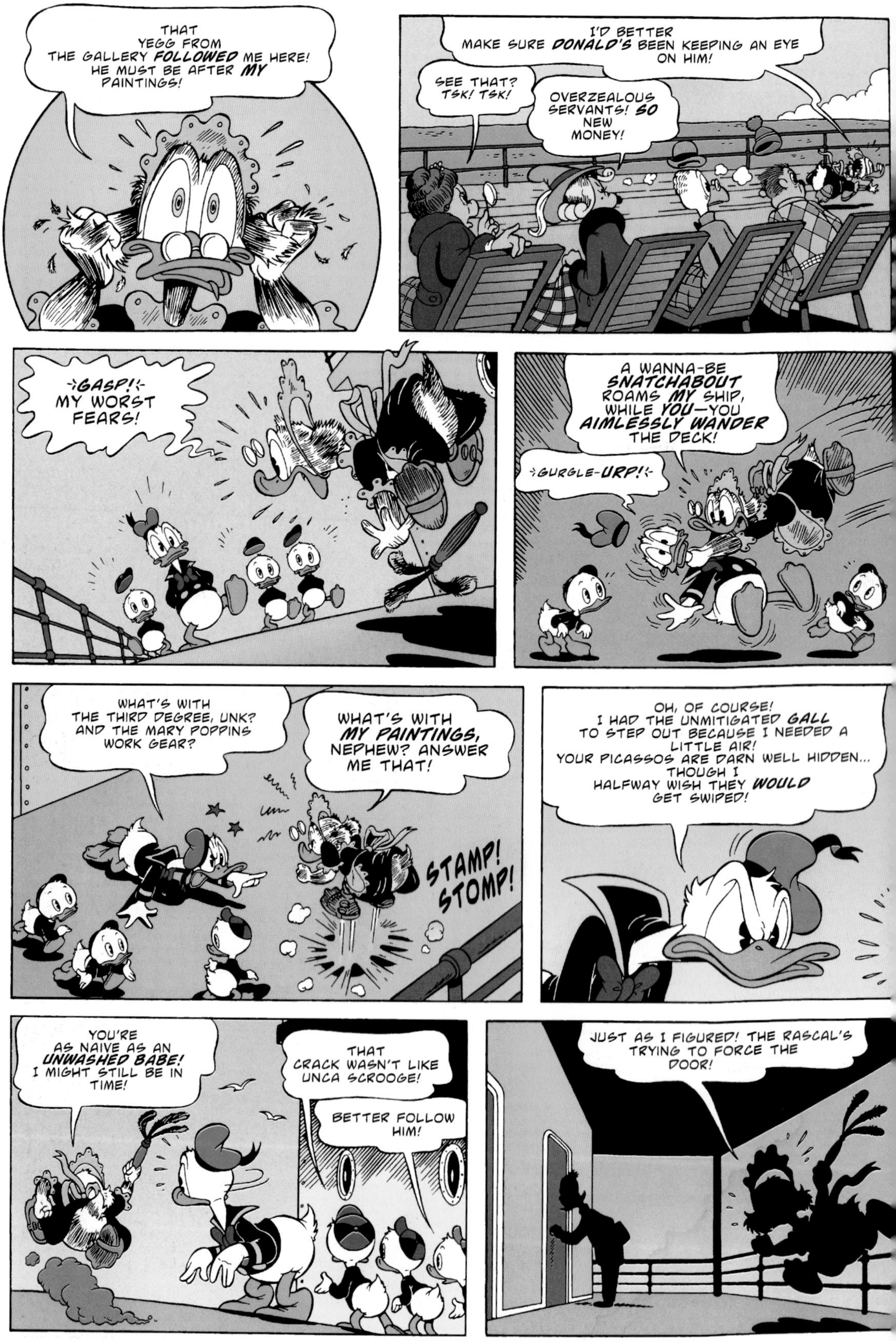
THAT YEGG FROM THE GALLERY FOLLOWED ME HERE! HE MUST BE AFTER MY PAINTINGS!
I'D BETTER MAKE SURE DONALD'S BEEN KEEPING AN EYE ON HIM!
SEE THAT? TSK! TSK!
OVERZEALOUS SERVANTS! SO NEW MONEY!
GASP! MY WORST FEARS!
A WANNA-BE SNATCHABOUT ROAMS MY SHIP, WHILE YOU—YOU AIMLESSLY WANDER THE DECK!
GURGLE-URP!
WHAT'S WITH THE THIRD DEGREE, UNK? AND THE MARY POPPINS WORK GEAR?
WHAT'S WITH MY PAINTINGS, NEPHEW? ANSWER ME THAT!
STAMP! STOMP!
OH, OF COURSE! I HAD THE UNMITIGATED GALL TO STEP OUT BECAUSE I NEEDED A LITTLE AIR! YOUR PICASSOS ARE DARN WELL HIDDEN... THOUGH I HALFWAY WISH THEY WOULD GET SWIPED!
YOU'RE AS NAIVE AS AN UNWASHED BABE! I MIGHT STILL BE IN TIME!
THAT CRACK WASN'T LIKE UNCA SCROOGE!
BETTER FOLLOW HIM!
JUST AS I FIGURED! THE RASCAL'S TRYING TO FORCE THE DOOR!

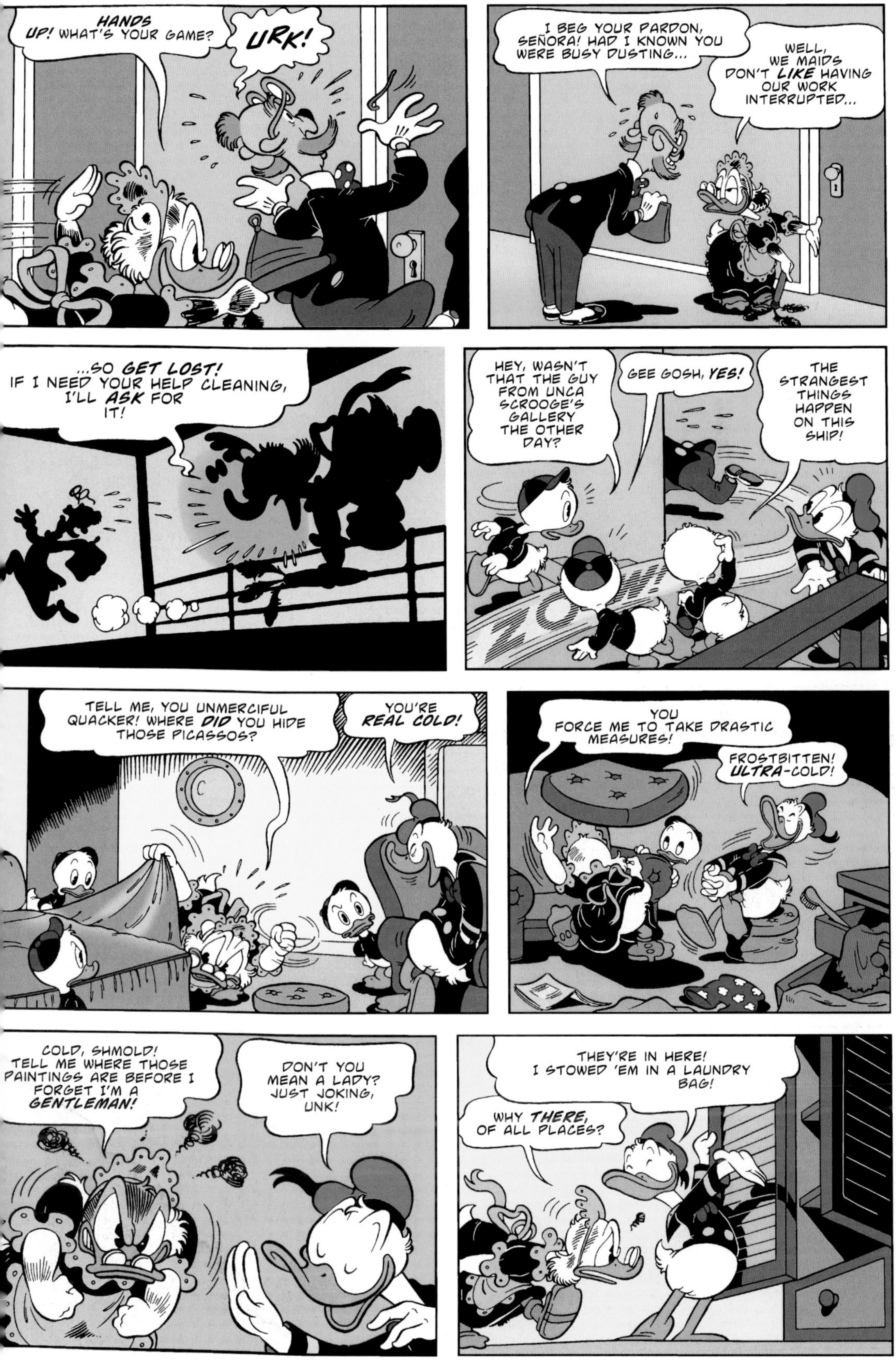
HANDS UP! WHAT'S YOUR GAME?
URK!
I BEG YOUR PARDON, SEÑORA! HAD I KNOWN YOU WERE BUSY DUSTING...
WELL, WE MAIDS DON'T LIKE HAVING OUR WORK INTERRUPTED...
...SO GET LOST! IF I NEED YOUR HELP CLEANING, I'LL ASK FOR IT!
HEY, WASN'T THAT THE GUY FROM UNCA SCROOGE'S GALLERY THE OTHER DAY?
GEE GOSH, YES!
THE STRANGEST THINGS HAPPEN ON THIS SHIP!
ZOOM!
TELL ME, YOU UNMERCIFUL QUACKER! WHERE DID YOU HIDE THOSE PICASSOS?
YOU'RE REAL COLD!
YOU FORCE ME TO TAKE DRASTIC MEASURES!
FROSTBITTEN! ULTRA-COLD!
COLD, SHMOLD! TELL ME WHERE THOSE PAINTINGS ARE BEFORE I FORGET I'M A GENTLEMAN!
DON'T YOU MEAN A LADY? JUST JOKING, UNK!
THEY'RE IN HERE! I STOWED 'EM IN A LAUNDRY BAG!
WHY THERE, OF ALL PLACES?

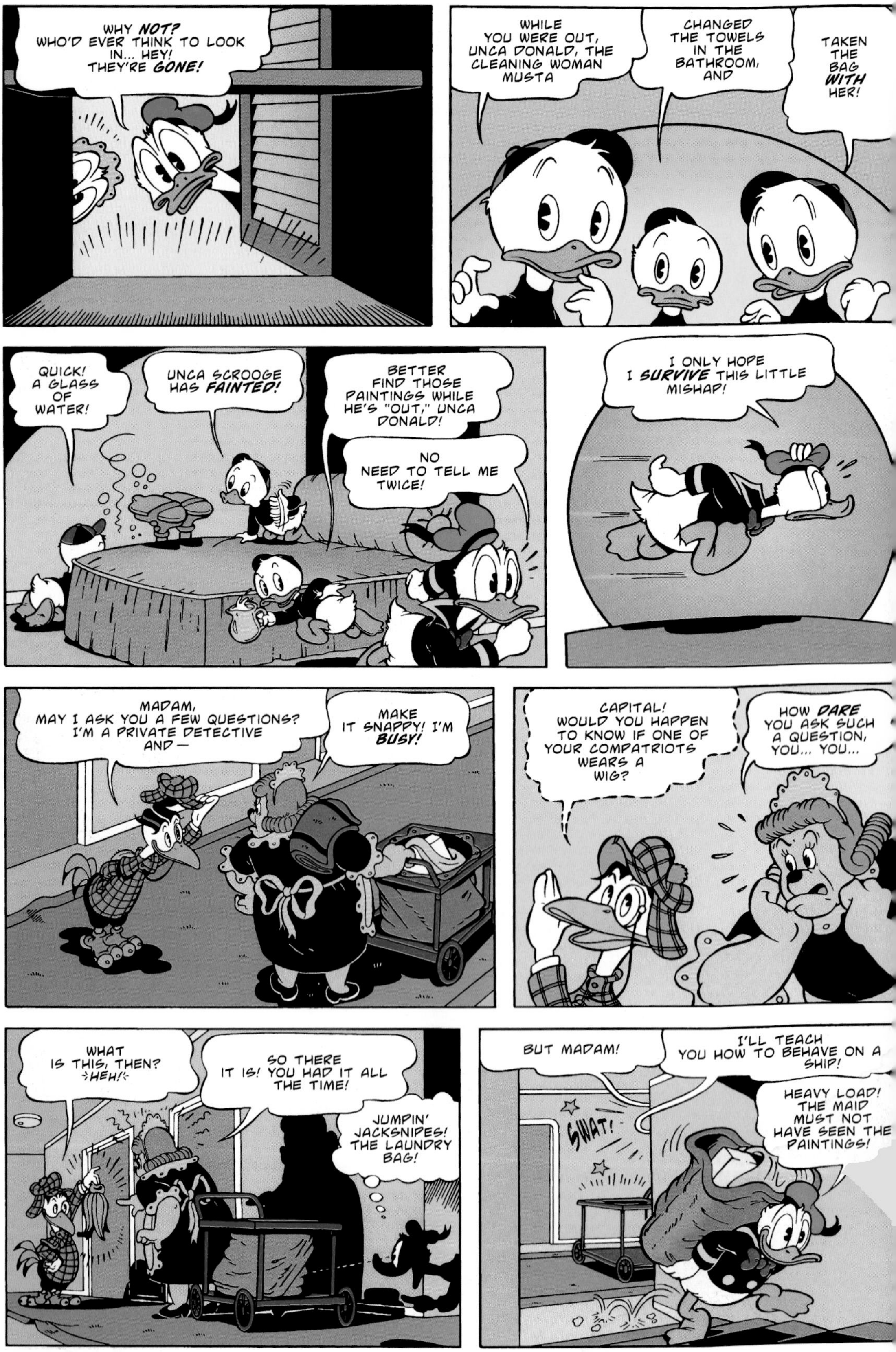
WHY NOT? WHO'D EVER THINK TO LOOK IN... HEY! THEY'RE GONE!
WHILE YOU WERE OUT, UNCA DONALD, THE CLEANING WOMAN MUSTA
CHANGED THE TOWELS IN THE BATHROOM, AND
TAKEN THE BAG WITH HER!
QUICK! A GLASS OF WATER!
UNCA SCROOGE HAS FAINTED!
BETTER FIND THOSE PAINTINGS WHILE HE'S "OUT," UNCA DONALD!
NO NEED TO TELL ME TWICE!
I ONLY HOPE I SURVIVE THIS LITTLE MISHAP!
MADAM, MAY I ASK YOU A FEW QUESTIONS? I'M A PRIVATE DETECTIVE AND—
MAKE IT SNAPPY! I'M BUSY!
CAPITAL! WOULD YOU HAPPEN TO KNOW IF ONE OF YOUR COMPATRIOTS WEARS A WIG?
HOW DARE YOU ASK SUCH A QUESTION, YOU... YOU...
WHAT IS THIS, THEN? ✧HEH!✧
SO THERE IT IS! YOU HAD IT ALL THE TIME!
JUMPIN' JACKSNIPES! THE LAUNDRY BAG!
BUT MADAM!
I'LL TEACH YOU HOW TO BEHAVE ON A SHIP!
SWAT!
HEAVY LOAD! THE MAID MUST NOT HAVE SEEN THE PAINTINGS!

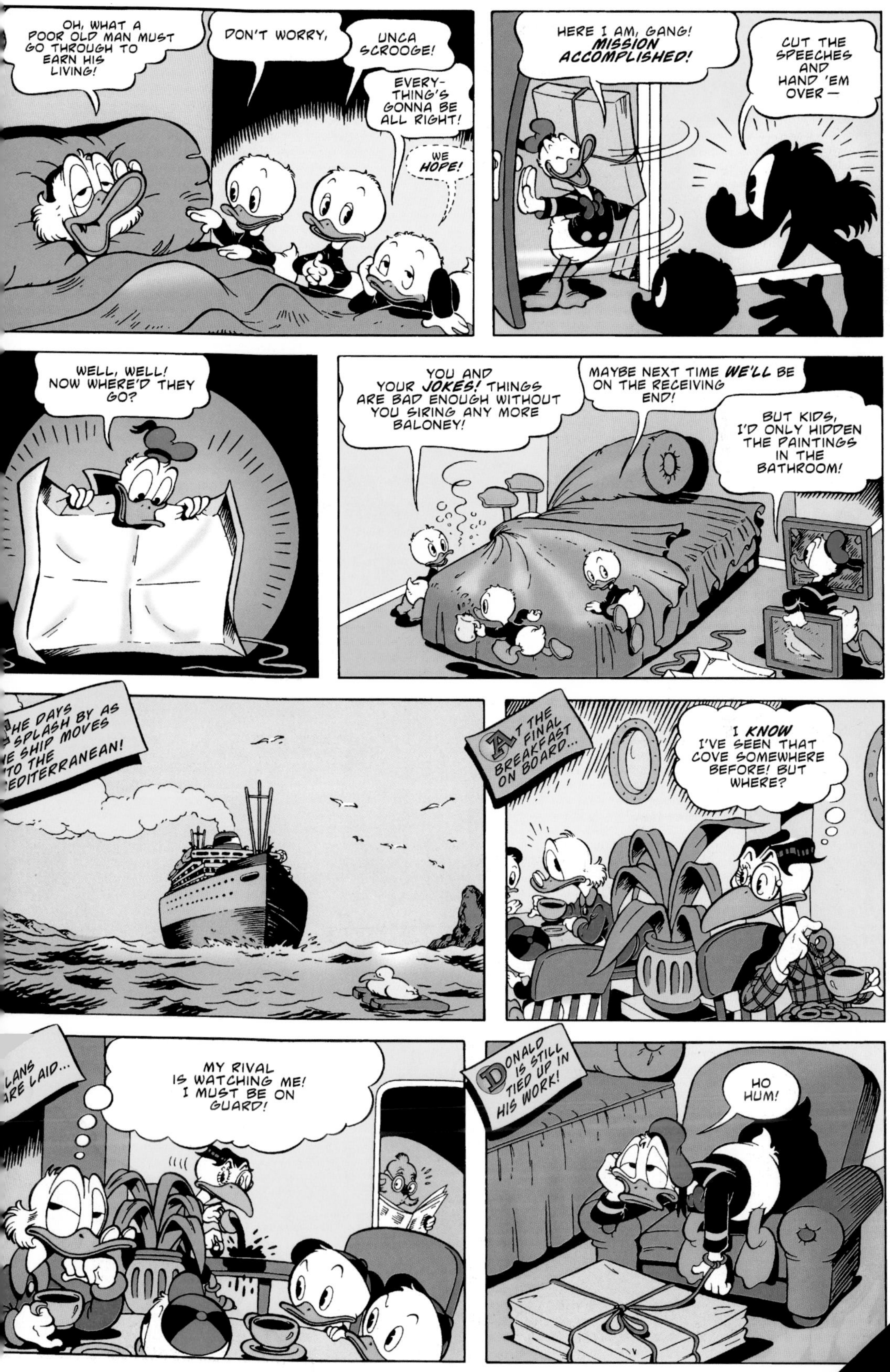
OH, WHAT A POOR OLD MAN MUST GO THROUGH TO EARN HIS LIVING!
DON'T WORRY,
UNCA SCROOGE!
EVERY-THING'S GONNA BE ALL RIGHT!
WE HOPE!
HERE I AM, GANG! MISSION ACCOMPLISHED!
CUT THE SPEECHES AND HAND 'EM OVER —
WELL, WELL! NOW WHERE'D THEY GO?
YOU AND YOUR JOKES! THINGS ARE BAD ENOUGH WITHOUT YOU SIRING ANY MORE BALONEY!
MAYBE NEXT TIME WE'LL BE ON THE RECEIVING END!
BUT KIDS, I'D ONLY HIDDEN THE PAINTINGS IN THE BATHROOM!
HE DAYS SPLASH BY AS E SHIP MOVES TO THE EDITERRANEAN!
AT THE FINAL BREAKFAST ON BOARD...
I KNOW I'VE SEEN THAT COVE SOMEWHERE BEFORE! BUT WHERE?
LANS ARE LAID...
MY RIVAL IS WATCHING ME! I MUST BE ON GUARD!
DONALD IS STILL TIED UP IN HIS WORK!
HO HUM!

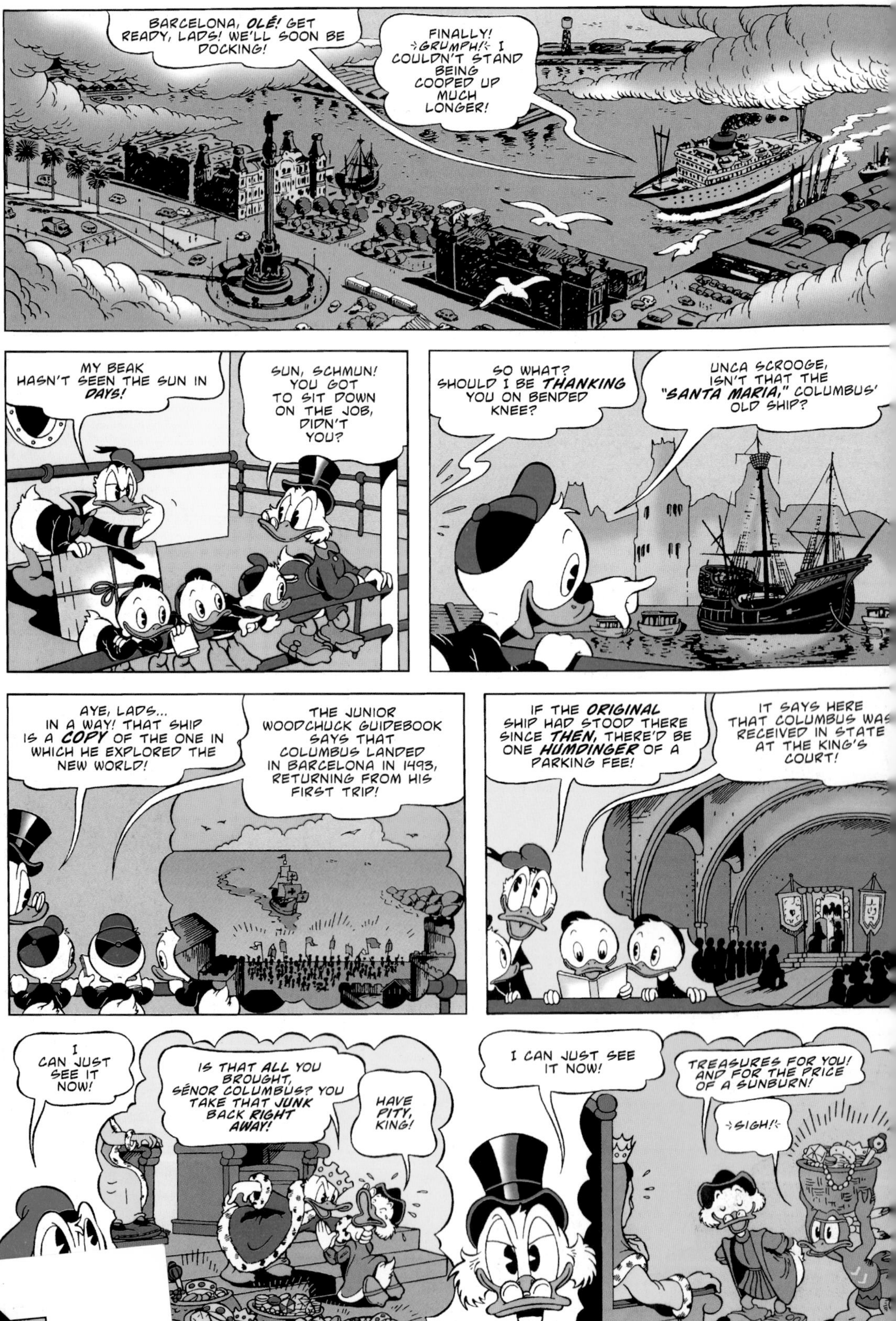

BARCELONA, OLÉ! GET READY, LADS! WE'LL SOON BE DOCKING!
FINALLY! GRUMPH! I COULDN'T STAND BEING COOPED UP MUCH LONGER!
MY BEAK HASN'T SEEN THE SUN IN DAYS!
SUN, SCHMUN! YOU GOT TO SIT DOWN ON THE JOB, DIDN'T YOU?
SO WHAT? SHOULD I BE THANKING YOU ON BENDED KNEE?
UNCA SCROOGE, ISN'T THAT THE "SANTA MARIA," COLUMBUS' OLD SHIP?
AYE, LADS... IN A WAY! THAT SHIP IS A COPY OF THE ONE IN WHICH HE EXPLORED THE NEW WORLD!
THE JUNIOR WOODCHUCK GUIDEBOOK SAYS THAT COLUMBUS LANDED IN BARCELONA IN 1493, RETURNING FROM HIS FIRST TRIP!
IF THE ORIGINAL SHIP HAD STOOD THERE SINCE THEN, THERE'D BE ONE HUMDINGER OF A PARKING FEE!
IT SAYS HERE THAT COLUMBUS WAS RECEIVED IN STATE AT THE KING'S COURT!
I CAN JUST SEE IT NOW!
IS THAT ALL YOU BROUGHT, SÉNOR COLUMBUS? YOU TAKE THAT JUNK BACK RIGHT AWAY!
HAVE PITY, KING!
I CAN JUST SEE IT NOW!
TREASURES FOR YOU! AND FOR THE PRICE OF A SUNBURN!
SIGH!

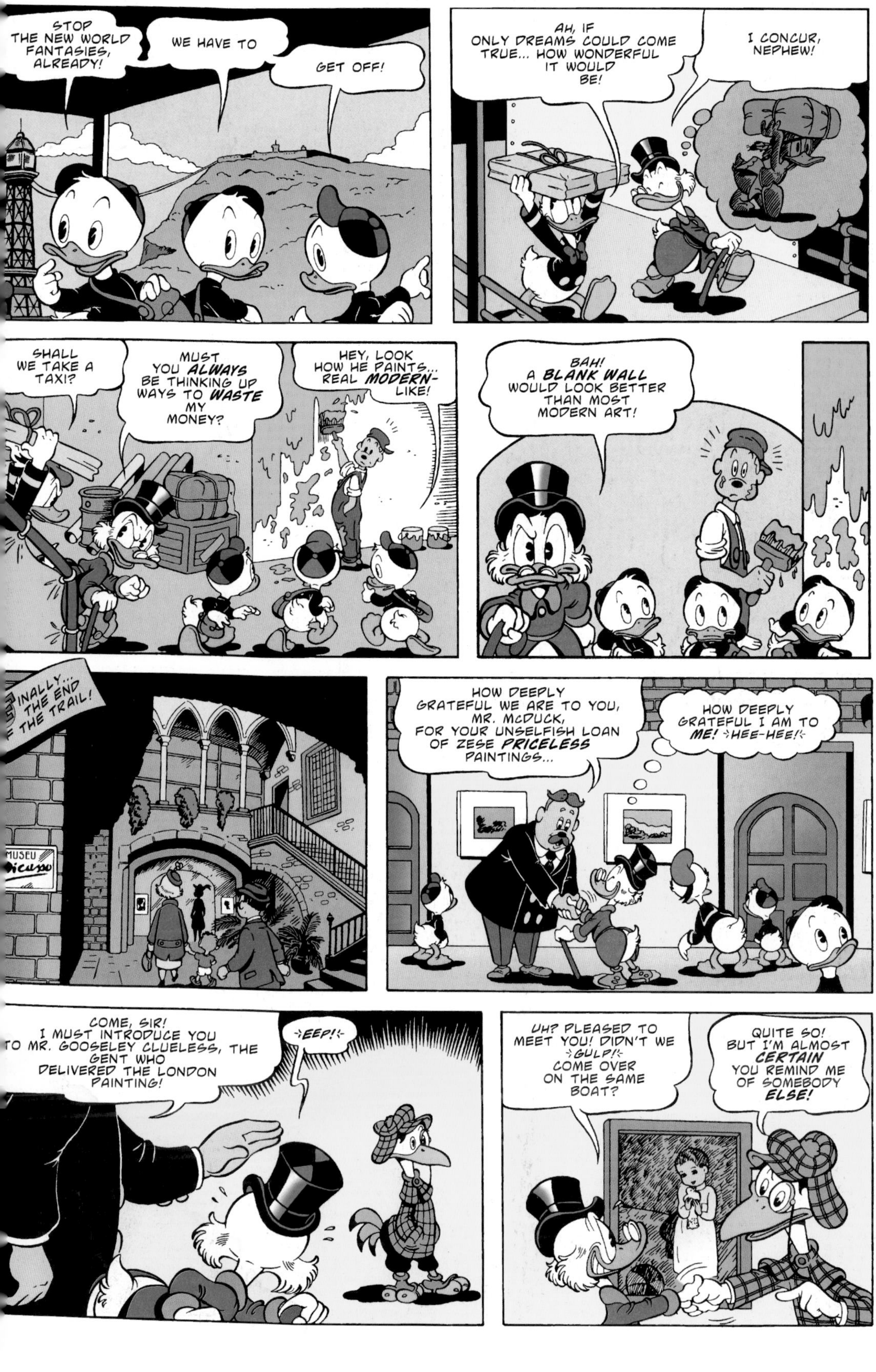
STOP THE NEW WORLD FANTASIES, ALREADY!
WE HAVE TO
GET OFF!
AH, IF ONLY DREAMS COULD COME TRUE... HOW WONDERFUL IT WOULD BE!
I CONCUR, NEPHEW!
SHALL WE TAKE A TAXI?
MUST YOU ALWAYS BE THINKING UP WAYS TO WASTE MY MONEY?
HEY, LOOK HOW HE PAINTS... REAL MODERN-LIKE!
BAH! A BLANK WALL WOULD LOOK BETTER THAN MOST MODERN ART!
FINALLY... THE END OF THE TRAIL!
MUSEU Picasso
HOW DEEPLY GRATEFUL WE ARE TO YOU, MR. McDUCK, FOR YOUR UNSELFISH LOAN OF ZESE PRICELESS PAINTINGS...
HOW DEEPLY GRATEFUL I AM TO ME! HEE-HEE!
COME, SIR! I MUST INTRODUCE YOU TO MR. GOOSELEY CLUELESS, THE GENT WHO DELIVERED THE LONDON PAINTING!
EEP!
UH? PLEASED TO MEET YOU! DIDN'T WE GULP! COME OVER ON THE SAME BOAT?
QUITE SO! BUT I'M ALMOST CERTAIN YOU REMIND ME OF SOMEBODY ELSE!

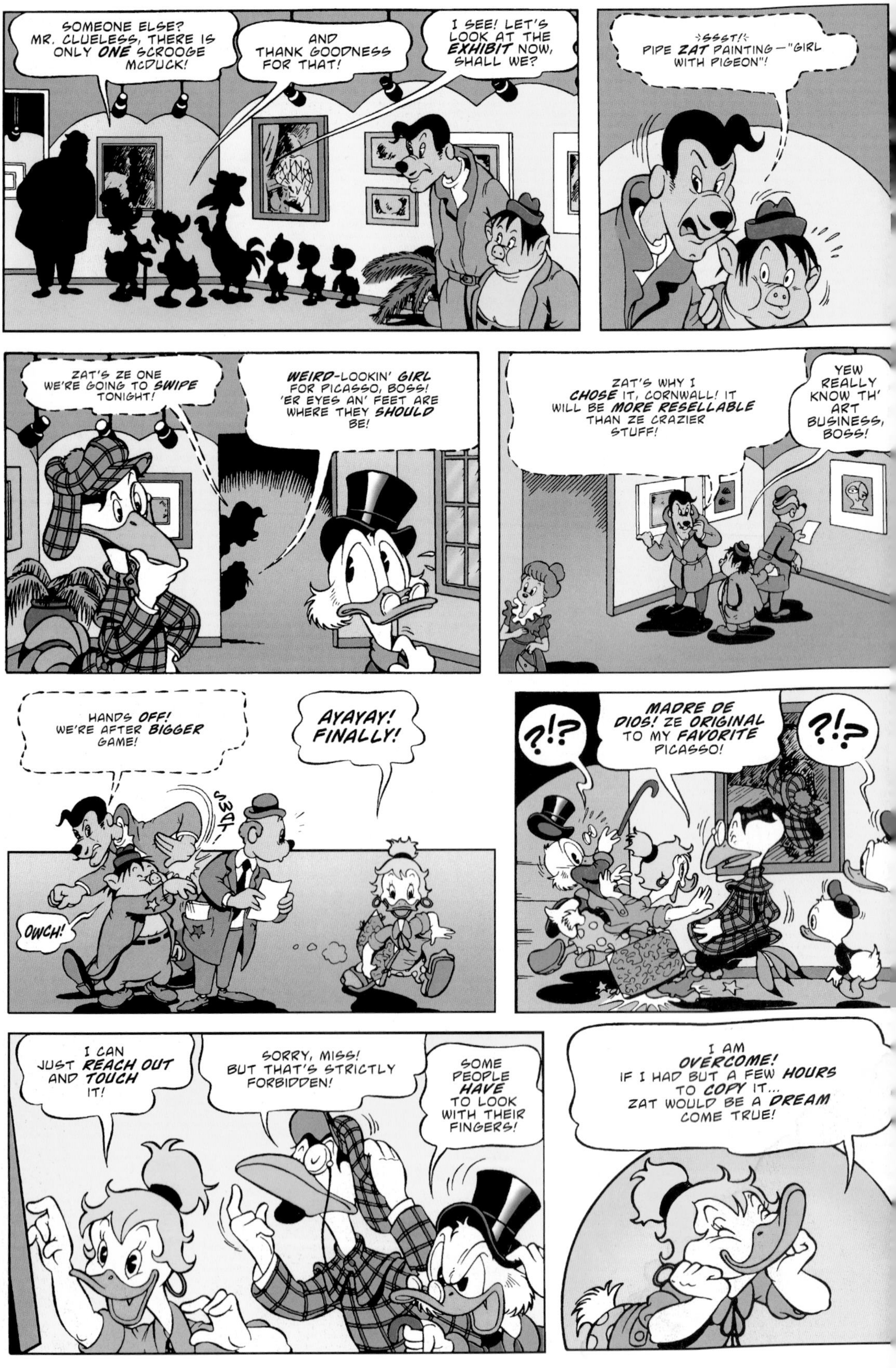

SOMEONE ELSE? MR. CLUELESS, THERE IS ONLY ONE SCROOGE McDUCK!
AND THANK GOODNESS FOR THAT!
I SEE! LET'S LOOK AT THE EXHIBIT NOW, SHALL WE?
-SSST!- PIPE ZAT PAINTING—"GIRL WITH PIGEON"!
ZAT'S ZE ONE WE'RE GOING TO SWIPE TONIGHT!
WEIRD-LOOKIN' GIRL FOR PICASSO, BOSS! 'ER EYES AN' FEET ARE WHERE THEY SHOULD BE!
ZAT'S WHY I CHOSE IT, CORNWALL! IT WILL BE MORE RESELLABLE THAN ZE CRAZIER STUFF!
YEW REALLY KNOW TH' ART BUSINESS, BOSS!
HANDS OFF! WE'RE AFTER BIGGER GAME!
SWAT
OWCH!
AYAYAY! FINALLY!
?!?
MADRE DE DIOS! ZE ORIGINAL TO MY FAVORITE PICASSO!
?!?
I CAN JUST REACH OUT AND TOUCH IT!
SORRY, MISS! BUT THAT'S STRICTLY FORBIDDEN!
SOME PEOPLE HAVE TO LOOK WITH THEIR FINGERS!
I AM OVERCOME! IF I HAD BUT A FEW HOURS TO COPY IT... ZAT WOULD BE A DREAM COME TRUE!

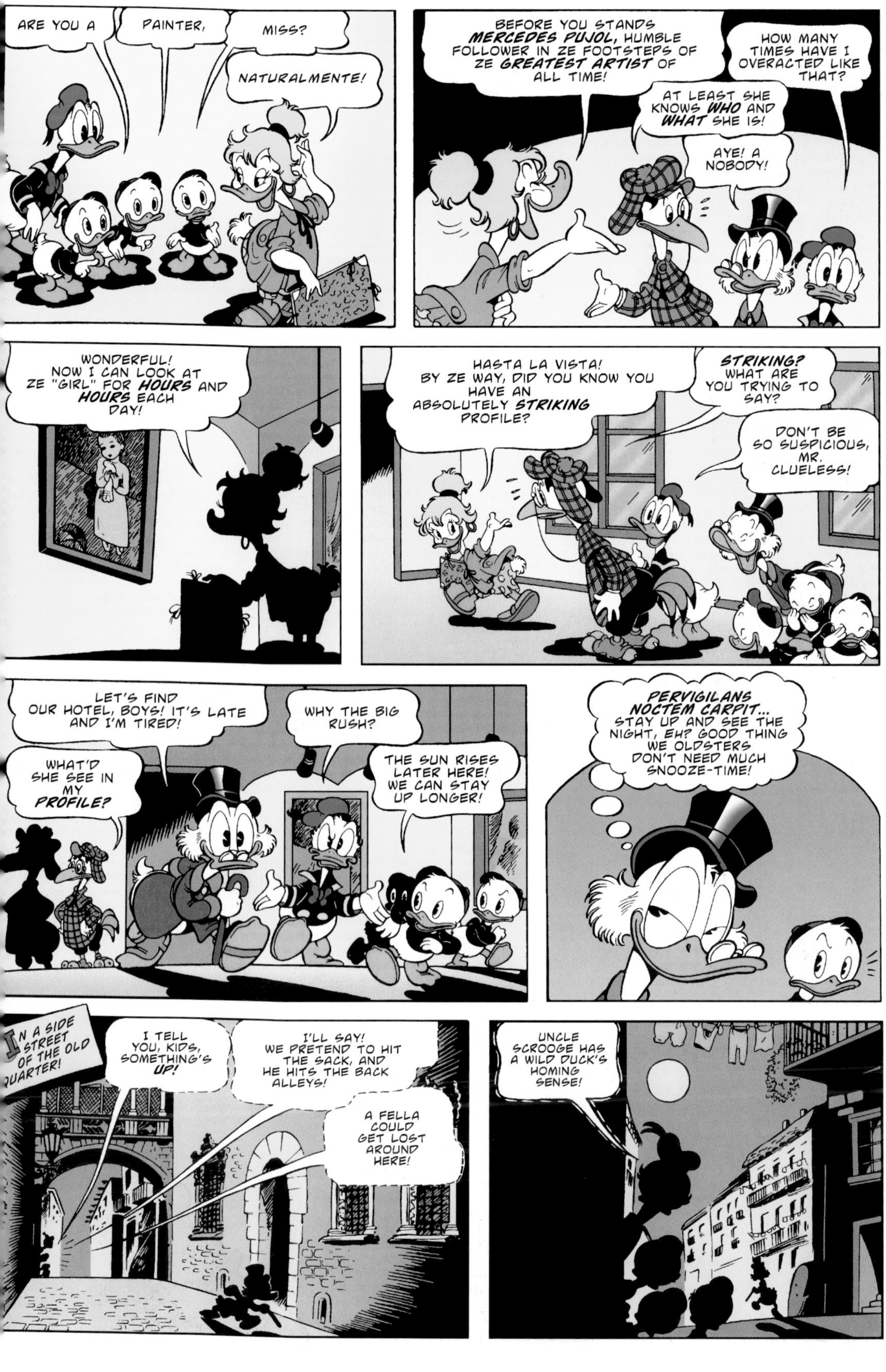
ARE YOU A
PAINTER,
MISS?
NATURALMENTE!
BEFORE YOU STANDS MERCEDES PUJOL, HUMBLE FOLLOWER IN ZE FOOTSTEPS OF ZE GREATEST ARTIST OF ALL TIME!
AT LEAST SHE KNOWS WHO AND WHAT SHE IS!
AYE! A NOBODY!
HOW MANY TIMES HAVE I OVERACTED LIKE THAT?
WONDERFUL! NOW I CAN LOOK AT ZE "GIRL" FOR HOURS AND HOURS EACH DAY!
HASTA LA VISTA! BY ZE WAY, DID YOU KNOW YOU HAVE AN ABSOLUTELY STRIKING PROFILE?
STRIKING? WHAT ARE YOU TRYING TO SAY?
DON'T BE SO SUSPICIOUS, MR. CLUELESS!
LET'S FIND OUR HOTEL, BOYS! IT'S LATE AND I'M TIRED!
WHAT'D SHE SEE IN MY PROFILE?
WHY THE BIG RUSH?
THE SUN RISES LATER HERE! WE CAN STAY UP LONGER!
PERVIGILANS NOCTEM CARPIT... STAY UP AND SEE THE NIGHT, EH? GOOD THING WE OLDSTERS DON'T NEED MUCH SNOOZE-TIME!
IN A SIDE STREET OF THE OLD QUARTER!
I TELL YOU, KIDS, SOMETHING'S UP!
I'LL SAY! WE PRETEND TO HIT THE SACK, AND HE HITS THE BACK ALLEYS!
A FELLA COULD GET LOST AROUND HERE!
UNCLE SCROOGE HAS A WILD DUCK'S HOMING SENSE!

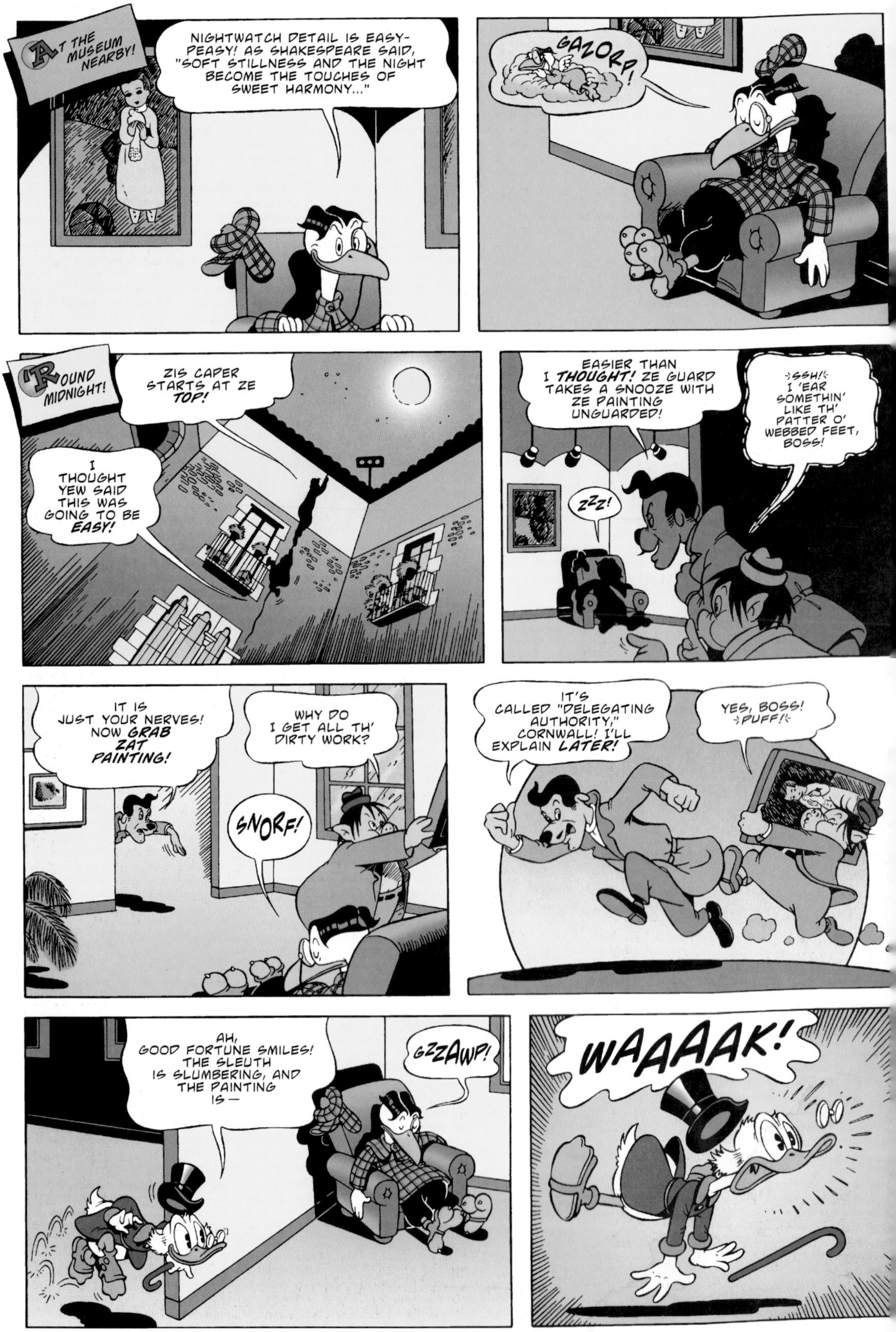

AT THE MUSEUM NEARBY!
NIGHTWATCH DETAIL IS EASY-PEASY! AS SHAKESPEARE SAID, "SOFT STILLNESS AND THE NIGHT BECOME THE TOUCHES OF SWEET HARMONY..."
GAZORP!
'ROUND MIDNIGHT!
ZIS CAPER STARTS AT ZE TOP!
I THOUGHT YEW SAID THIS WAS GOING TO BE EASY!
EASIER THAN I THOUGHT! ZE GUARD TAKES A SNOOZE WITH ZE PAINTING UNGUARDED!
ZZZ!
SSH! I 'EAR SOMETHIN' LIKE TH' PATTER O' WEBBED FEET, BOSS!
IT IS JUST YOUR NERVES! NOW GRAB ZAT PAINTING!
WHY DO I GET ALL TH' DIRTY WORK?
SNORF!
IT'S CALLED "DELEGATING AUTHORITY," CORNWALL! I'LL EXPLAIN LATER!
YES, BOSS! PUFF!
AH, GOOD FORTUNE SMILES! THE SLEUTH IS SLUMBERING, AND THE PAINTING IS—
GZZAWP!
WAAAAK!

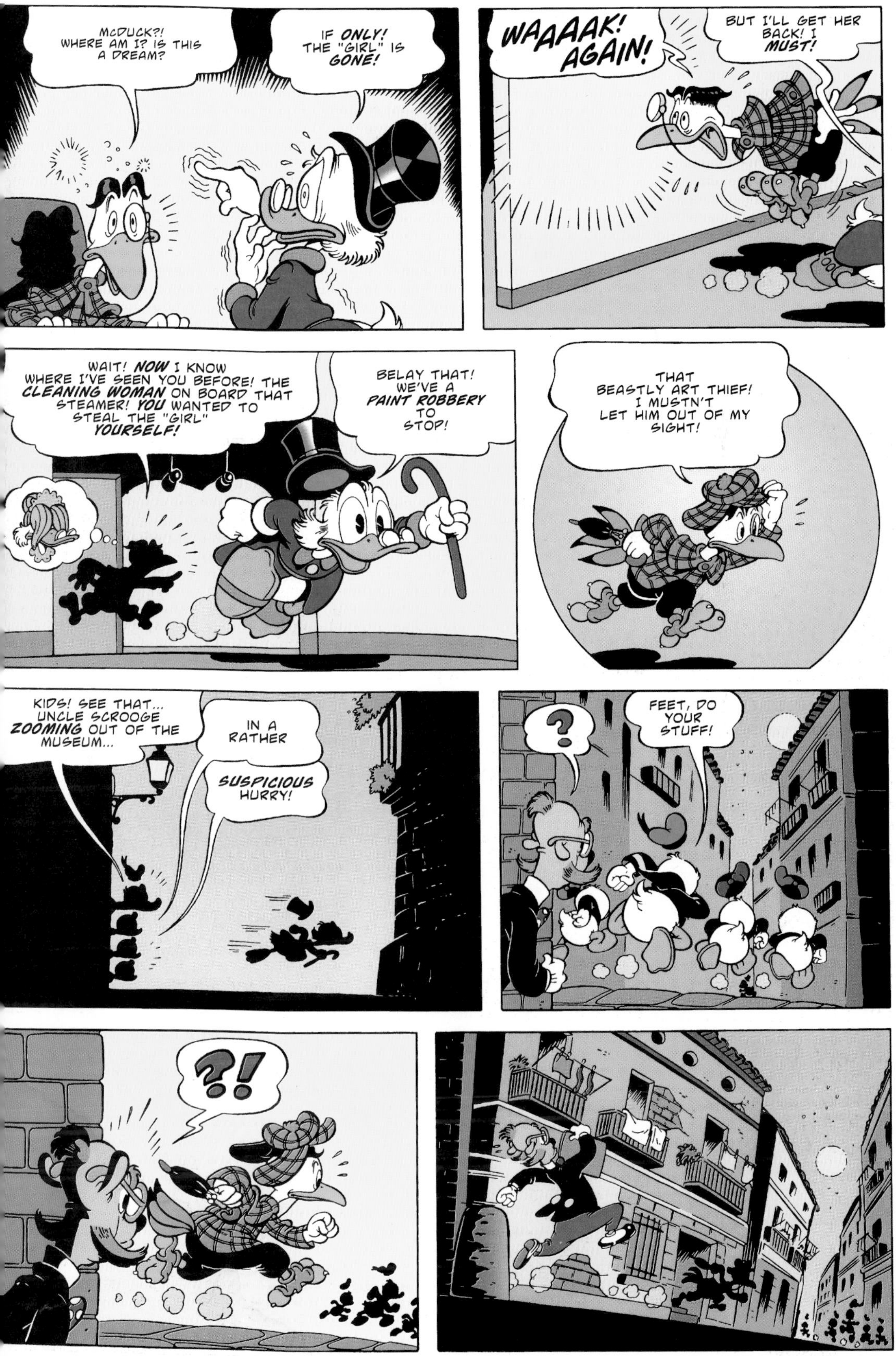
McDUCK?! WHERE AM I? IS THIS A DREAM?
IF ONLY! THE "GIRL" IS GONE!
WAAAAK! AGAIN!
BUT I'LL GET HER BACK! I MUST!
WAIT! NOW I KNOW WHERE I'VE SEEN YOU BEFORE! THE CLEANING WOMAN ON BOARD THAT STEAMER! YOU WANTED TO STEAL THE "GIRL" YOURSELF!
BELAY THAT! WE'VE A PAINT ROBBERY TO STOP!
THAT BEASTLY ART THIEF! I MUSTN'T LET HIM OUT OF MY SIGHT!
KIDS! SEE THAT... UNCLE SCROOGE ZOOMING OUT OF THE MUSEUM...
IN A RATHER
SUSPICIOUS HURRY!
?
FEET, DO YOUR STUFF!
?!

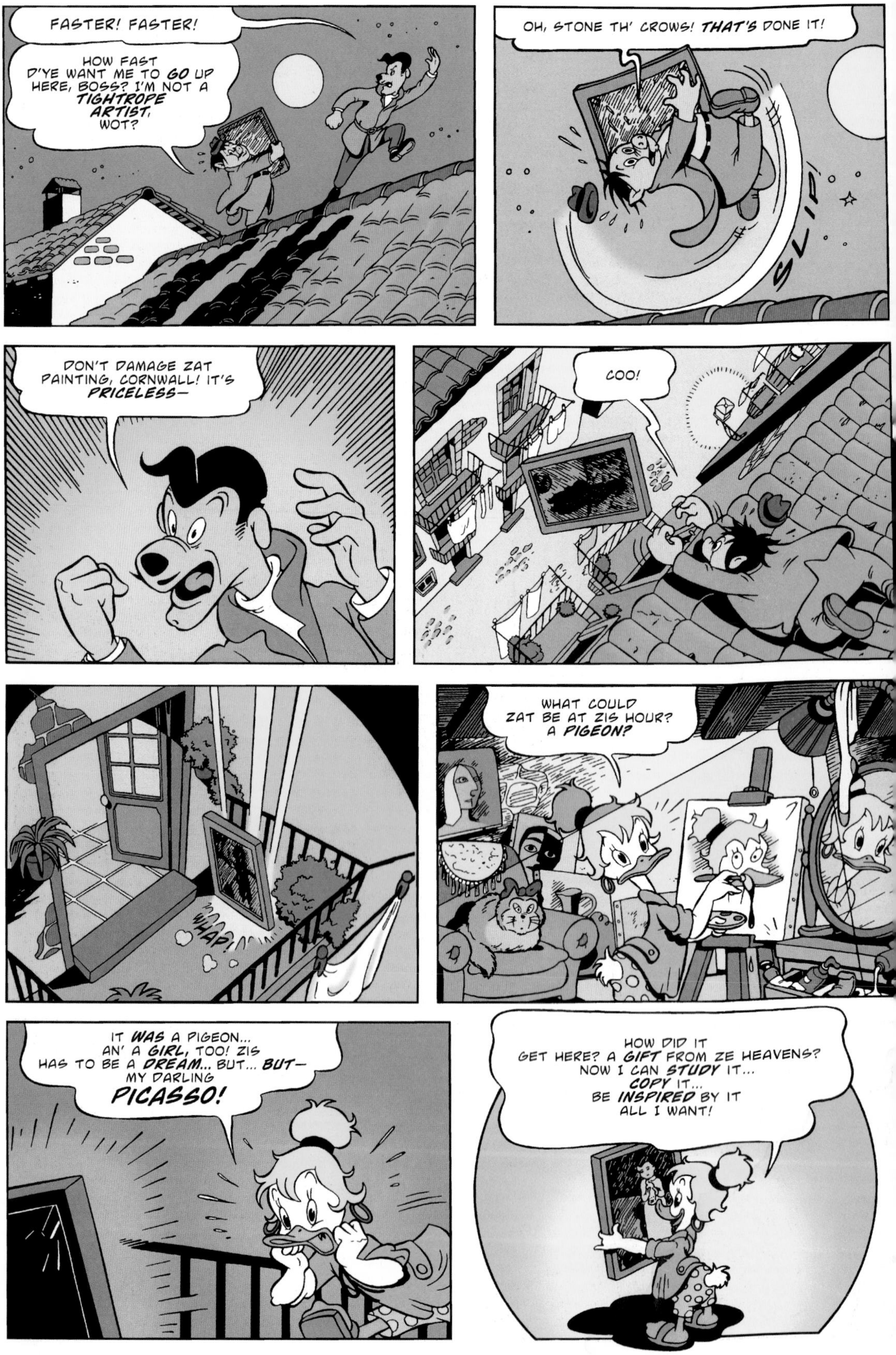
FASTER! FASTER!
HOW FAST D'YE WANT ME TO GO UP HERE, BOSS? I'M NOT A TIGHTROPE ARTIST, WOT?
OH, STONE TH' CROWS! THAT'S DONE IT!
SLIP!
DON'T DAMAGE ZAT PAINTING, CORNWALL! IT'S PRICELESS—
COO!
WHAP!
WHAT COULD ZAT BE AT ZIS HOUR? A PIGEON?
IT WAS A PIGEON... AN' A GIRL, TOO! ZIS HAS TO BE A DREAM... BUT... BUT— MY DARLING PICASSO!
HOW DID IT GET HERE? A GIFT FROM ZE HEAVENS? NOW I CAN STUDY IT... COPY IT... BE INSPIRED BY IT ALL I WANT!

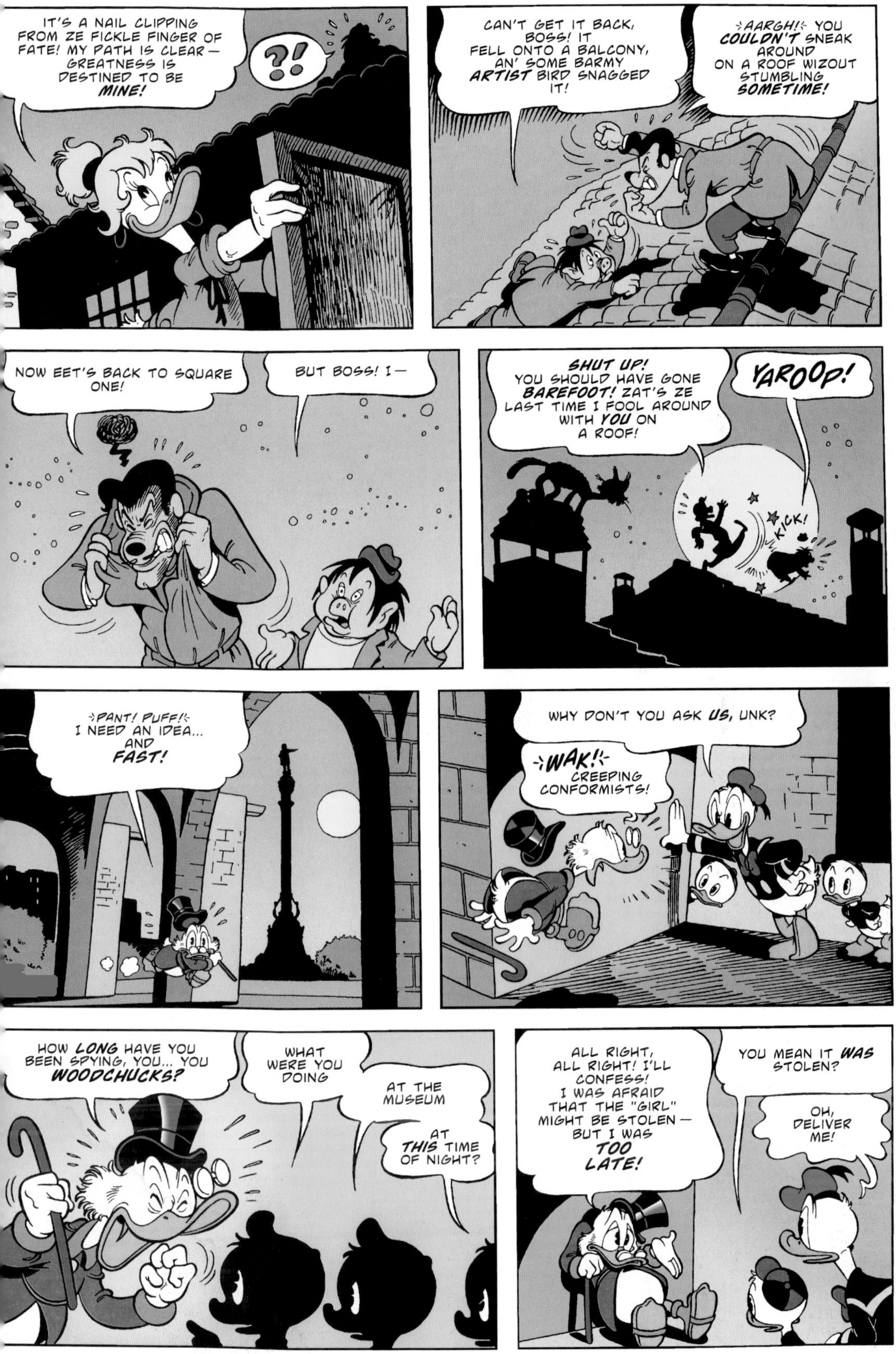
IT'S A NAIL CLIPPING FROM ZE FICKLE FINGER OF FATE! MY PATH IS CLEAR — GREATNESS IS DESTINED TO BE MINE!
?!
CAN'T GET IT BACK, BOSS! IT FELL ONTO A BALCONY, AN' SOME BARMY ARTIST BIRD SNAGGED IT!
AARGH! YOU COULDN'T SNEAK AROUND ON A ROOF WIZOUT STUMBLING SOMETIME!
NOW EET'S BACK TO SQUARE ONE!
BUT BOSS! I —
SHUT UP! YOU SHOULD HAVE GONE BAREFOOT! ZAT'S ZE LAST TIME I FOOL AROUND WITH YOU ON A ROOF!
YAROOP!
KICK!
PANT! PUFF! I NEED AN IDEA... AND FAST!
WHY DON'T YOU ASK US, UNK?
WAK! CREEPING CONFORMISTS!
HOW LONG HAVE YOU BEEN SPYING, YOU... YOU WOODCHUCKS?
WHAT WERE YOU DOING
AT THE MUSEUM
AT THIS TIME OF NIGHT?
ALL RIGHT, ALL RIGHT! I'LL CONFESS! I WAS AFRAID THAT THE "GIRL" MIGHT BE STOLEN — BUT I WAS TOO LATE!
YOU MEAN IT WAS STOLEN?
OH, DELIVER ME!

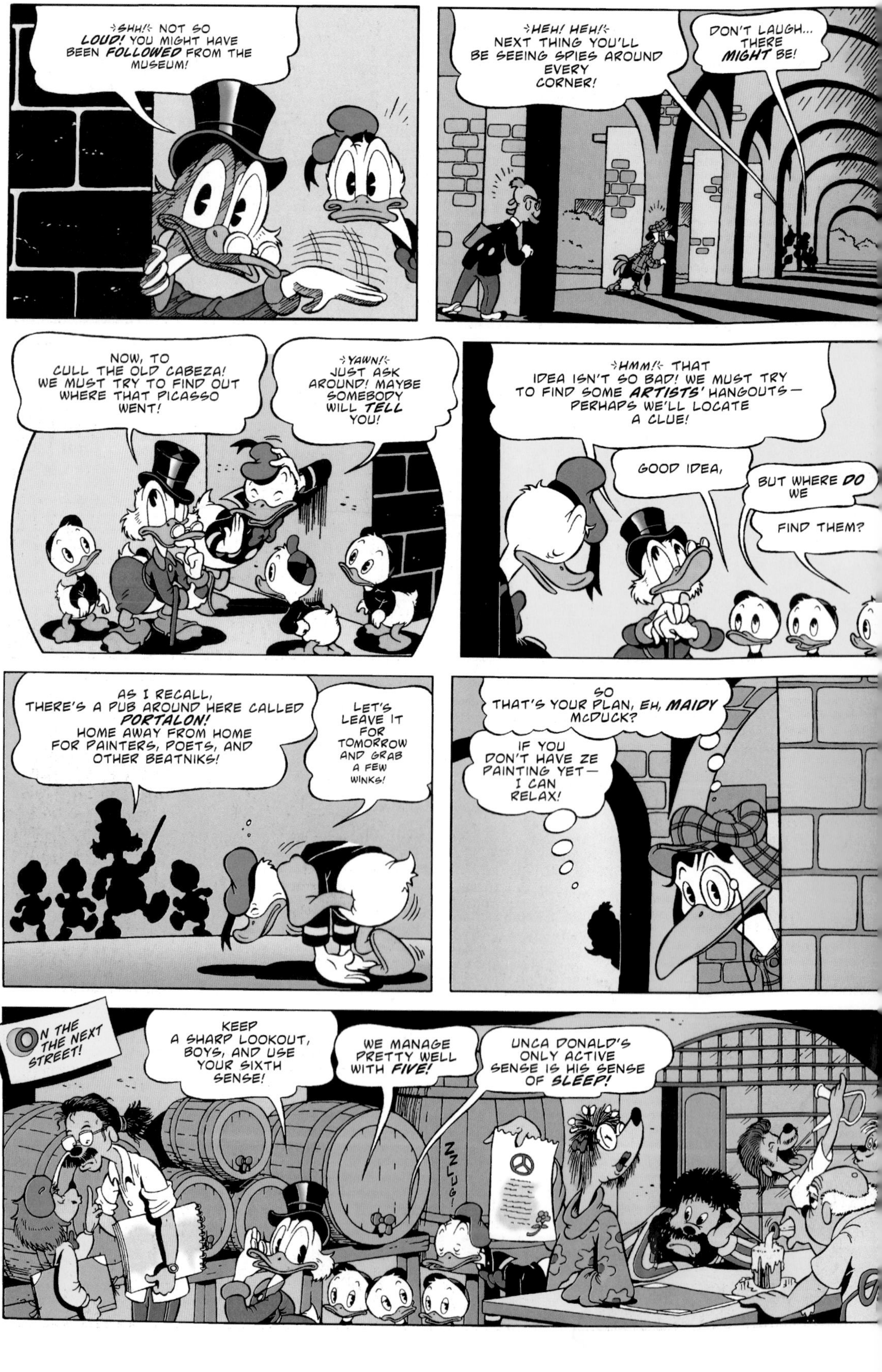

SHH! NOT SO LOUD! YOU MIGHT HAVE BEEN FOLLOWED FROM THE MUSEUM!
HEH! HEH! NEXT THING YOU'LL BE SEEING SPIES AROUND EVERY CORNER!
DON'T LAUGH... THERE MIGHT BE!
NOW, TO CULL THE OLD CABEZA! WE MUST TRY TO FIND OUT WHERE THAT PICASSO WENT!
YAWN! JUST ASK AROUND! MAYBE SOMEBODY WILL TELL YOU!
HMM! THAT IDEA ISN'T SO BAD! WE MUST TRY TO FIND SOME ARTISTS' HANGOUTS— PERHAPS WE'LL LOCATE A CLUE!
GOOD IDEA,
BUT WHERE DO WE
FIND THEM?
AS I RECALL, THERE'S A PUB AROUND HERE CALLED PORTALON! HOME AWAY FROM HOME FOR PAINTERS, POETS, AND OTHER BEATNIKS!
LET'S LEAVE IT FOR TOMORROW AND GRAB A FEW WINKS!
SO THAT'S YOUR PLAN, EH, MAIDY McDUCK?
IF YOU DON'T HAVE ZE PAINTING YET— I CAN RELAX!
ON THE THE NEXT STREET!
KEEP A SHARP LOOKOUT, BOYS, AND USE YOUR SIXTH SENSE!
WE MANAGE PRETTY WELL WITH FIVE!
UNCA DONALD'S ONLY ACTIVE SENSE IS HIS SENSE OF SLEEP!
ZZLUG!

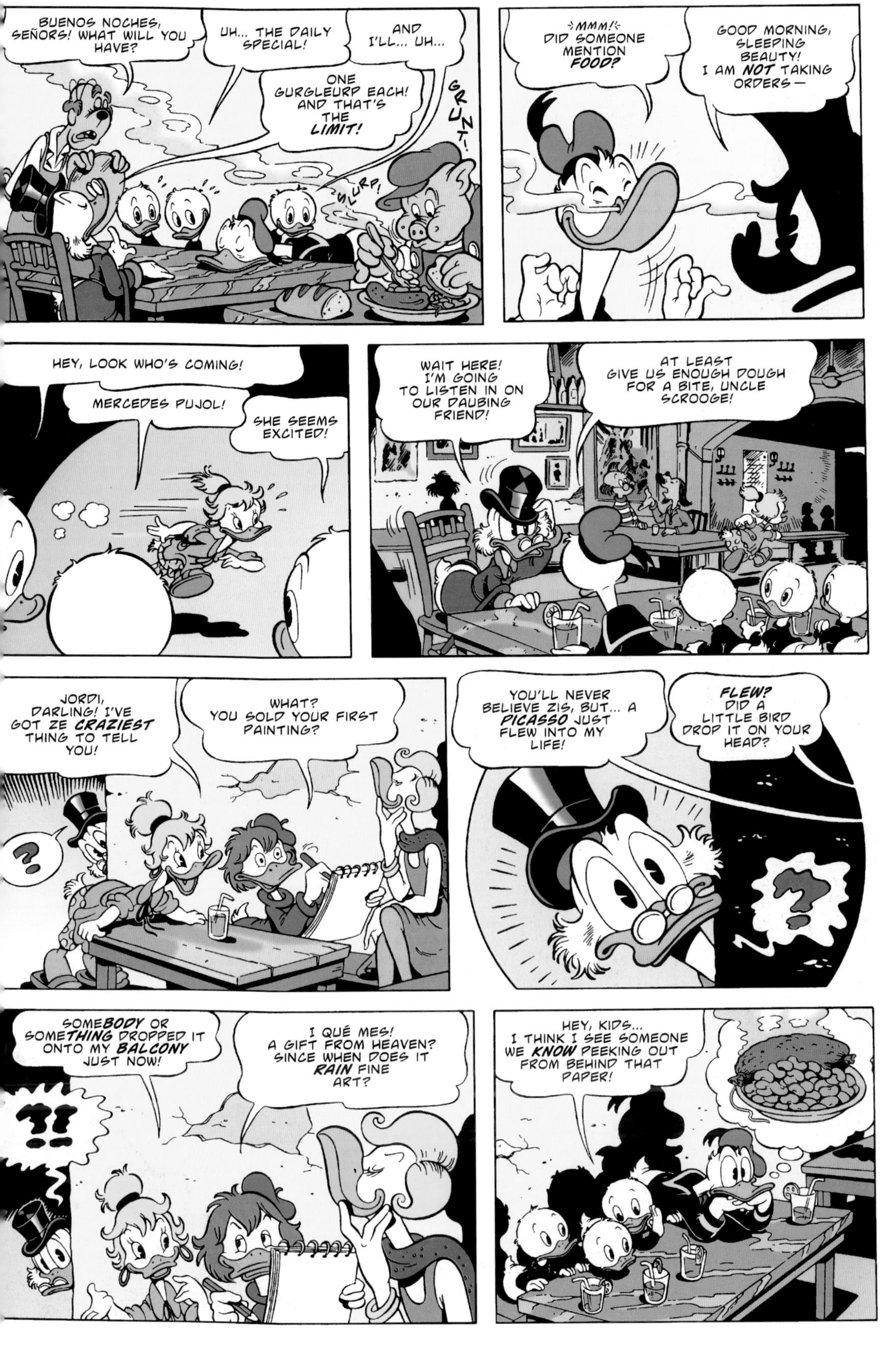

BUENOS NOCHES, SEÑORS! WHAT WILL YOU HAVE?
UH... THE DAILY SPECIAL!
AND I'LL... UH...
ONE GURGLEURP EACH! AND THAT'S THE LIMIT!
GRUNT!
SLURP!
MMM! DID SOMEONE MENTION FOOD?
GOOD MORNING, SLEEPING BEAUTY! I AM NOT TAKING ORDERS—
HEY, LOOK WHO'S COMING!
MERCEDES PUJOL!
SHE SEEMS EXCITED!
WAIT HERE! I'M GOING TO LISTEN IN ON OUR DAUBING FRIEND!
AT LEAST GIVE US ENOUGH DOUGH FOR A BITE, UNCLE SCROOGE!
JORDI, DARLING! I'VE GOT ZE CRAZIEST THING TO TELL YOU!
WHAT? YOU SOLD YOUR FIRST PAINTING?
?
YOU'LL NEVER BELIEVE ZIS, BUT... A PICASSO JUST FLEW INTO MY LIFE!
FLEW? DID A LITTLE BIRD DROP IT ON YOUR HEAD?
?
SOMEBODY OR SOMETHING DROPPED IT ONTO MY BALCONY JUST NOW!
I QUÉ MES! A GIFT FROM HEAVEN? SINCE WHEN DOES IT RAIN FINE ART?
?!
HEY, KIDS... I THINK I SEE SOMEONE WE KNOW PEEKING OUT FROM BEHIND THAT PAPER!

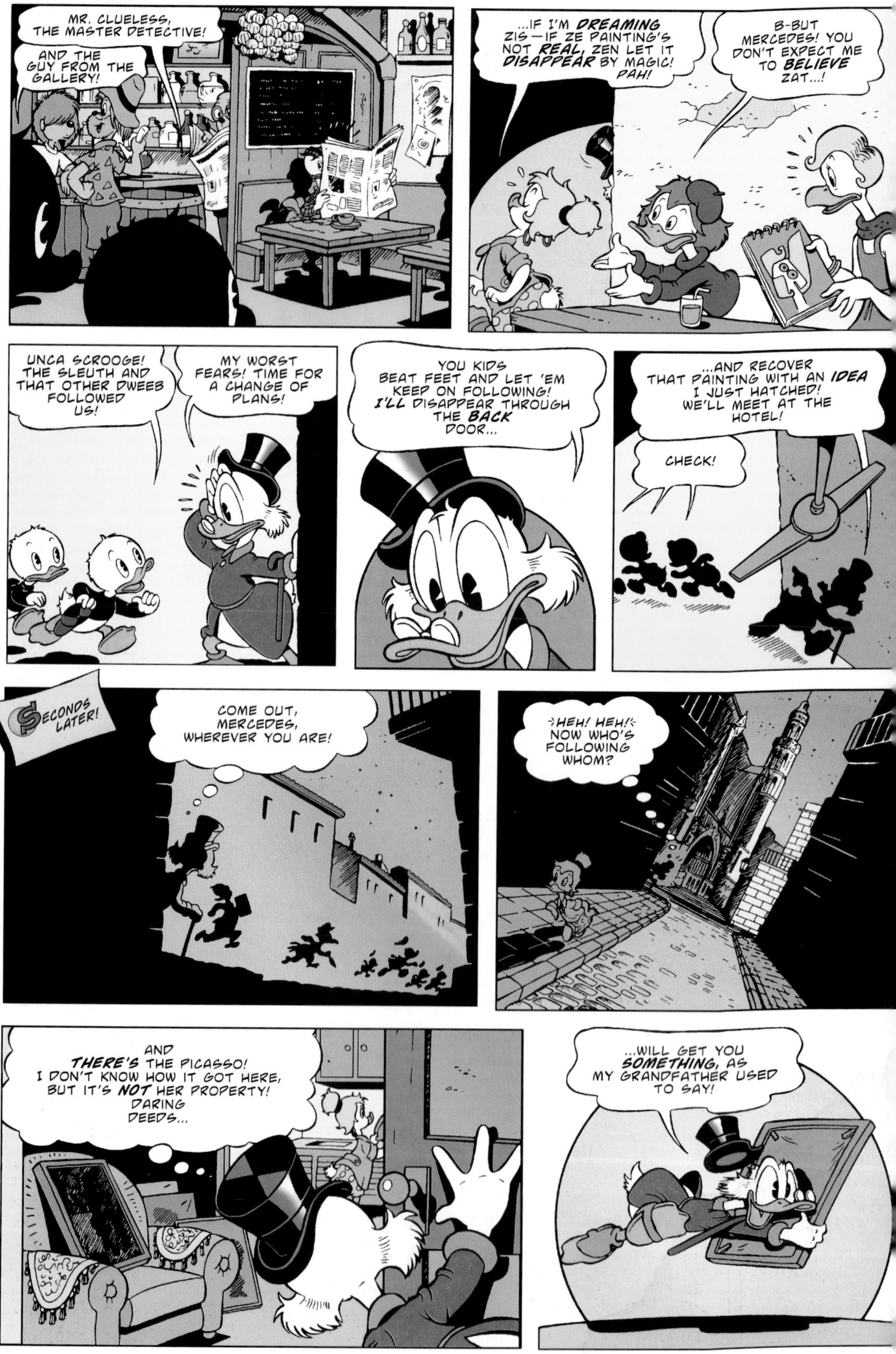
MR. CLUELESS, THE MASTER DETECTIVE!
AND THE GUY FROM THE GALLERY!
...IF I'M DREAMING ZIS—IF ZE PAINTING'S NOT REAL, ZEN LET IT DISAPPEAR BY MAGIC! PAH!
B-BUT MERCEDES! YOU DON'T EXPECT ME TO BELIEVE ZAT...!
UNCA SCROOGE! THE SLEUTH AND THAT OTHER DWEEB FOLLOWED US!
MY WORST FEARS! TIME FOR A CHANGE OF PLANS!
YOU KIDS BEAT FEET AND LET 'EM KEEP ON FOLLOWING! I'LL DISAPPEAR THROUGH THE BACK DOOR...
...AND RECOVER THAT PAINTING WITH AN IDEA I JUST HATCHED! WE'LL MEET AT THE HOTEL!
CHECK!
SECONDS LATER!
COME OUT, MERCEDES, WHEREVER YOU ARE!
HEH! HEH! NOW WHO'S FOLLOWING WHOM?
AND THERE'S THE PICASSO! I DON'T KNOW HOW IT GOT HERE, BUT IT'S NOT HER PROPERTY! DARING DEEDS...
...WILL GET YOU SOMETHING, AS MY GRANDFATHER USED TO SAY!

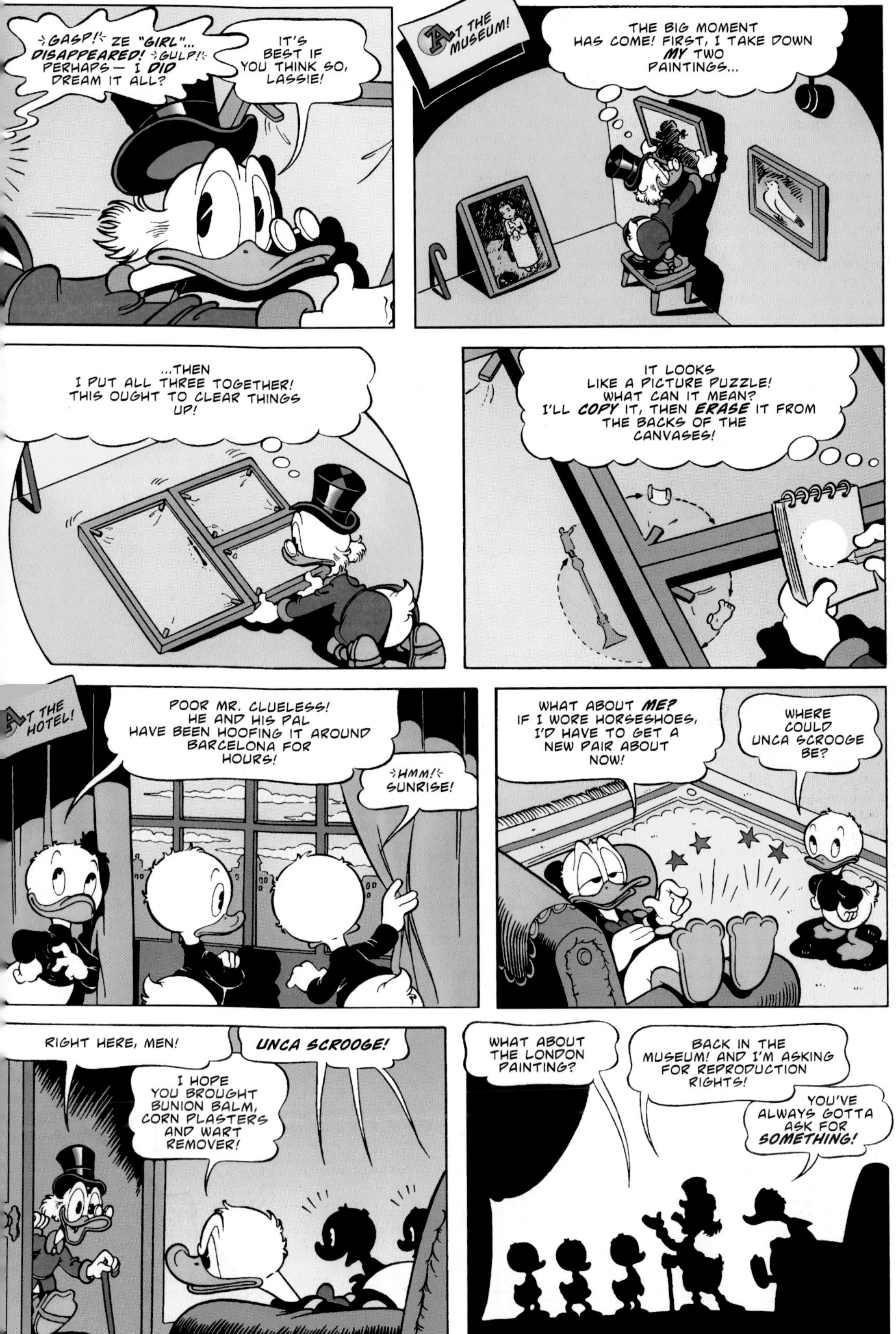
GASP! ZE "GIRL"... DISAPPEARED! GULP! PERHAPS— I DID DREAM IT ALL?
IT'S BEST IF YOU THINK SO, LASSIE!
AT THE MUSEUM!
THE BIG MOMENT HAS COME! FIRST, I TAKE DOWN MY TWO PAINTINGS...
...THEN I PUT ALL THREE TOGETHER! THIS OUGHT TO CLEAR THINGS UP!
IT LOOKS LIKE A PICTURE PUZZLE! WHAT CAN IT MEAN? I'LL COPY IT, THEN ERASE IT FROM THE BACKS OF THE CANVASES!
AT THE HOTEL!
POOR MR. CLUELESS! HE AND HIS PAL HAVE BEEN HOOFING IT AROUND BARCELONA FOR HOURS!
HMM! SUNRISE!
WHAT ABOUT ME? IF I WORE HORSESHOES, I'D HAVE TO GET A NEW PAIR ABOUT NOW!
WHERE COULD UNCA SCROOGE BE?
RIGHT HERE, MEN!
UNCA SCROOGE!
I HOPE YOU BROUGHT BUNION BALM, CORN PLASTERS AND WART REMOVER!
WHAT ABOUT THE LONDON PAINTING?
BACK IN THE MUSEUM! AND I'M ASKING FOR REPRODUCTION RIGHTS!
YOU'VE ALWAYS GOTTA ASK FOR SOMETHING!

OUR NEXT STEP IS TO DECODE *THESE* SYMBOLS! THEN WE MAY *REALLY* BE ONTO SOMETHING BIG!

HOW BIG? DROP A HINT, SHERLOCK!

LET *US* TRY, UNCA SCROOGE!

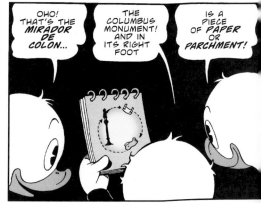

OHO! THAT'S THE *MIRADOR DE COLON*...

THE COLUMBUS MONUMENT! AND IN ITS RIGHT FOOT

IS A PIECE OF *PAPER* OR *PARCHMENT*!

GREAT, LADS! WITHOUT YOU I'D HAVE COME TO GRIEF! YOU REMIND ME OF *ME* IN MY YOUTH!

YOU WERE *YOUNG* ONCE? I DON'T BELIEVE IT!

TO THE BOTTOM OF LA RAMBLA, NEPHEWS! WE'RE "SHOE" TO FIND SOMETHING IN COLUMBUS' FOOT!

CAN'T WE NOD OUR NOODLES FOR AN INSTANT? MY *FOOT* IS *KILLING* ME!

WHY'S THIS LIFT CAR SO *CRAMPED?* A DUCK COULD GET *CLAUSTROPHOBIA!*

ALWAYS GRUMBLING, EH, DONALD? CUT THE YAMMER!

I CAN'T *TAKE* IT ANYMORE! ÷CHOKE!÷ I NEED *SUNSHINE* AND *FRESH AIR!*

WHEN WE REACH THE TOP YOU'LL HAVE PLENTY!

BEAUTIFUL *VIEW*, EH, LADS?

YOU SAID IT!

OWOOO, I'M *SICK!* MY STOMACH'S TURNING FLITTER-FLOPS!

BUT YOUR LUNGS AND TONGUE ARE A-1, OLD SON!

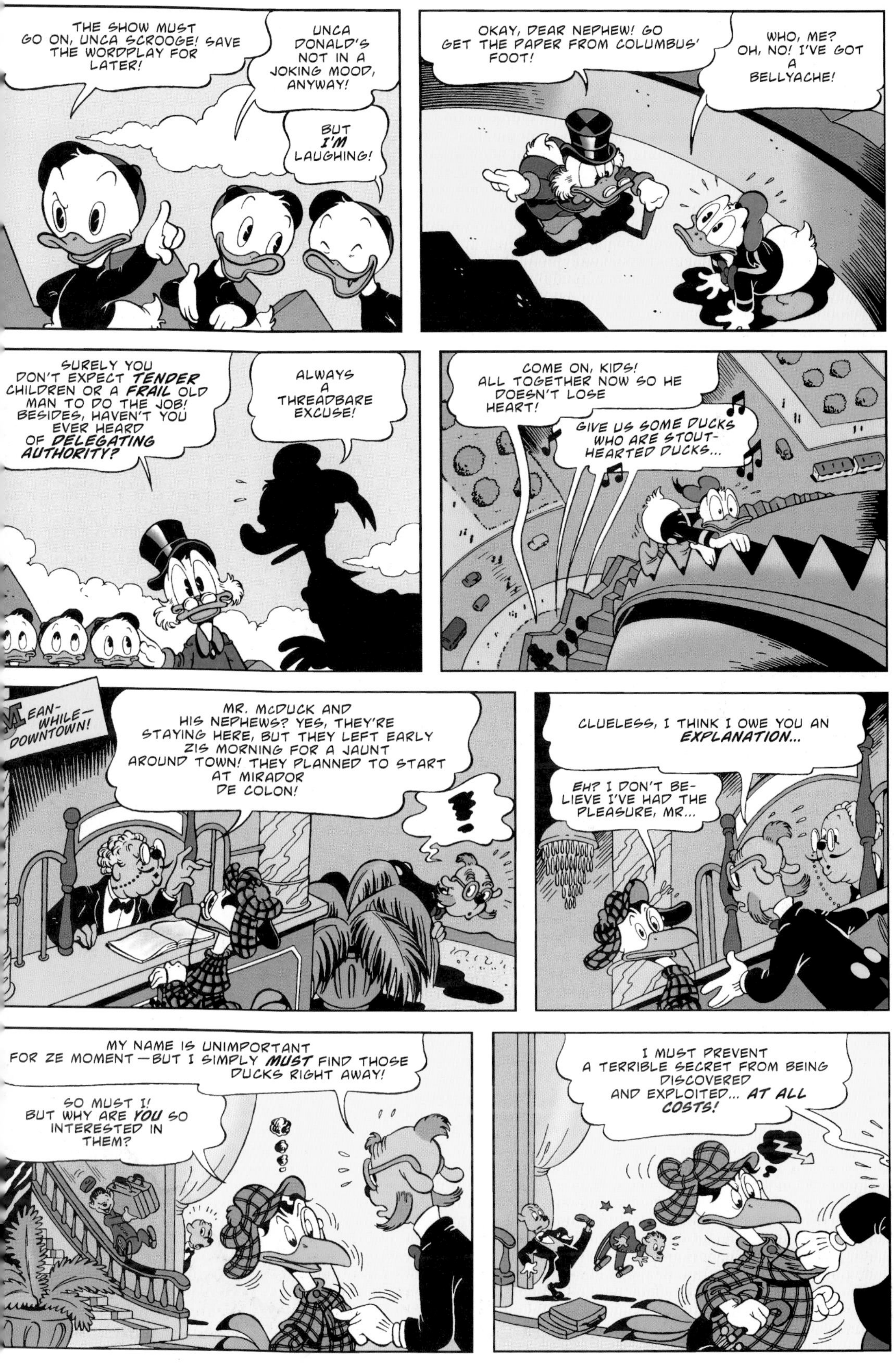
THE SHOW MUST GO ON, UNCA SCROOGE! SAVE THE WORDPLAY FOR LATER!
UNCA DONALD'S NOT IN A JOKING MOOD, ANYWAY!
BUT I'M LAUGHING!
OKAY, DEAR NEPHEW! GO GET THE PAPER FROM COLUMBUS' FOOT!
WHO, ME? OH, NO! I'VE GOT A BELLYACHE!
SURELY YOU DON'T EXPECT TENDER CHILDREN OR A FRAIL OLD MAN TO DO THE JOB! BESIDES, HAVEN'T YOU EVER HEARD OF DELEGATING AUTHORITY?
ALWAYS A THREADBARE EXCUSE!
COME ON, KIDS! ALL TOGETHER NOW SO HE DOESN'T LOSE HEART!
GIVE US SOME DUCKS WHO ARE STOUT-HEARTED DUCKS...
MEANWHILE— DOWNTOWN!
MR. McDUCK AND HIS NEPHEWS? YES, THEY'RE STAYING HERE, BUT THEY LEFT EARLY ZIS MORNING FOR A JAUNT AROUND TOWN! THEY PLANNED TO START AT MIRADOR DE COLON!
CLUELESS, I THINK I OWE YOU AN EXPLANATION...
EH? I DON'T BE-LIEVE I'VE HAD THE PLEASURE, MR...
MY NAME IS UNIMPORTANT FOR ZE MOMENT—BUT I SIMPLY MUST FIND THOSE DUCKS RIGHT AWAY!
SO MUST I! BUT WHY ARE YOU SO INTERESTED IN THEM?
I MUST PREVENT A TERRIBLE SECRET FROM BEING DISCOVERED AND EXPLOITED... AT ALL COSTS!

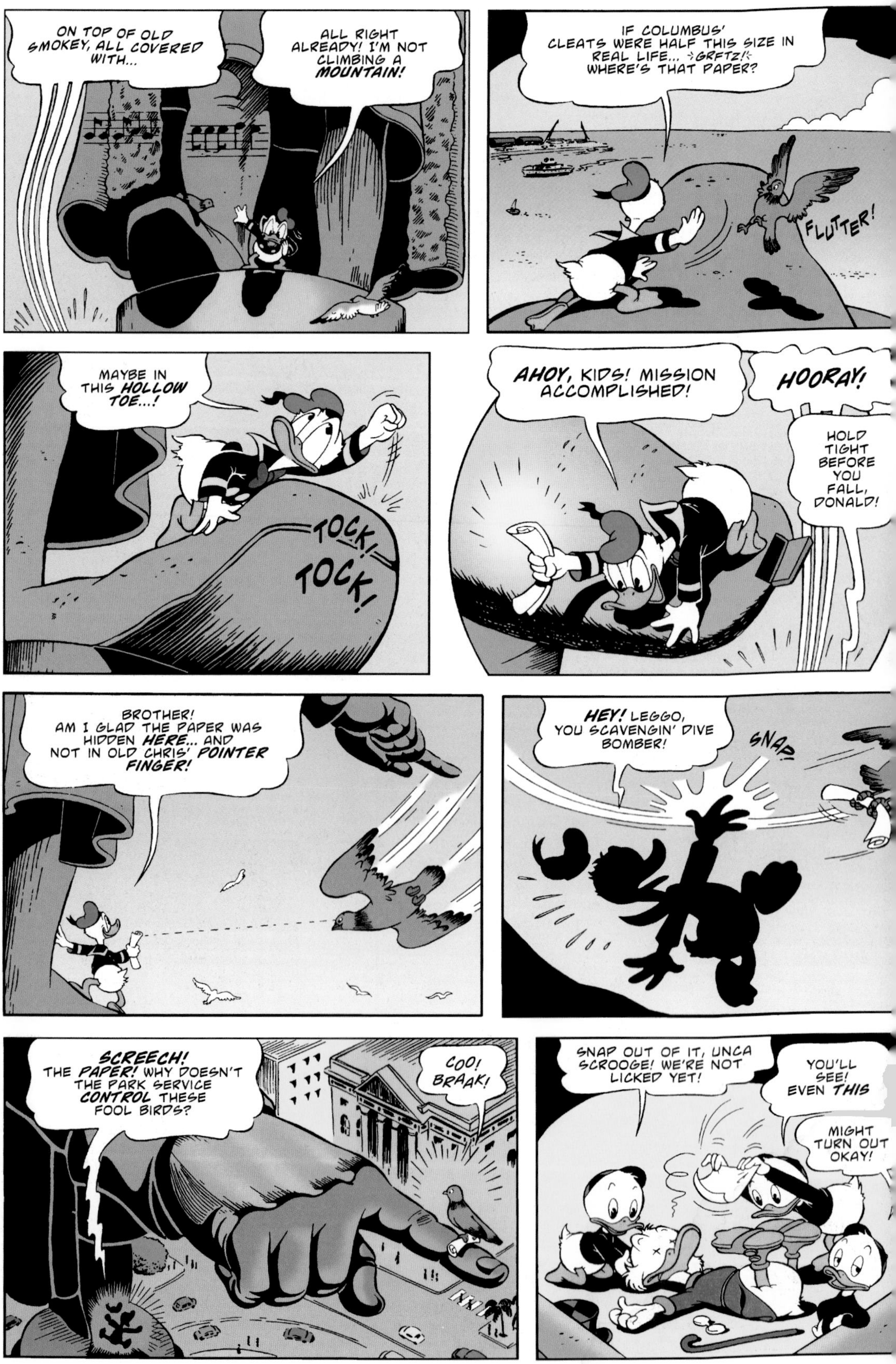
ON TOP OF OLD SMOKEY, ALL COVERED WITH...
ALL RIGHT ALREADY! I'M NOT CLIMBING A MOUNTAIN!
IF COLUMBUS' CLEATS WERE HALF THIS SIZE IN REAL LIFE... GRFTZ! WHERE'S THAT PAPER?
FLUTTER!
MAYBE IN THIS HOLLOW TOE...!
TOCK! TOCK!
AHOY, KIDS! MISSION ACCOMPLISHED!
HOORAY!
HOLD TIGHT BEFORE YOU FALL, DONALD!
BROTHER! AM I GLAD THE PAPER WAS HIDDEN HERE... AND NOT IN OLD CHRIS' POINTER FINGER!
HEY! LEGGO, YOU SCAVENGIN' DIVE BOMBER!
SNAP!
SCREECH! THE PAPER! WHY DOESN'T THE PARK SERVICE CONTROL THESE FOOL BIRDS?
COO! BRAAK!
SNAP OUT OF IT, UNCA SCROOGE! WE'RE NOT LICKED YET!
YOU'LL SEE! EVEN THIS
MIGHT TURN OUT OKAY!

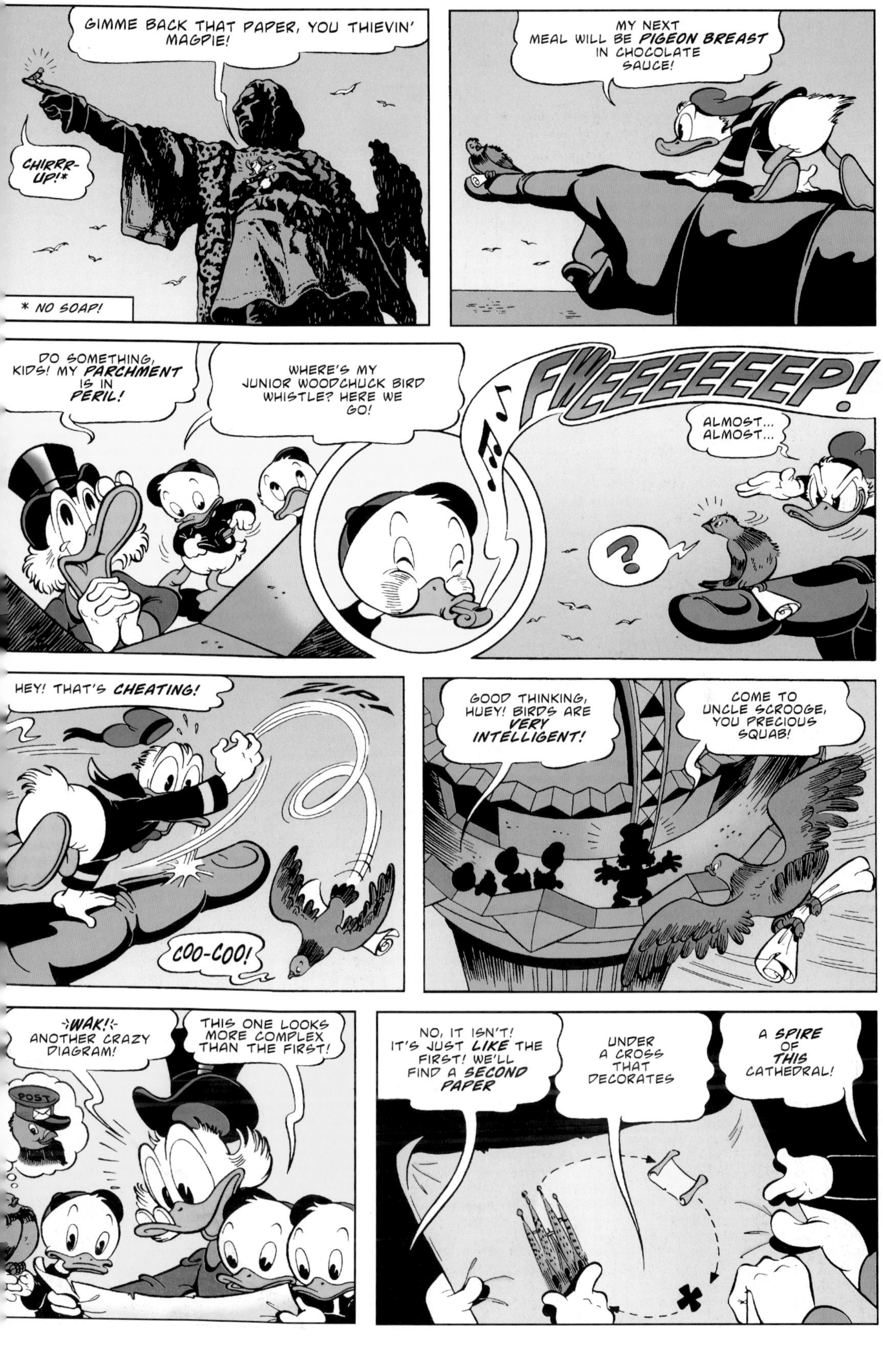
GIMME BACK THAT PAPER, YOU THIEVIN' MAGPIE!
CHIRRR-UP!*
* NO SOAP!
MY NEXT MEAL WILL BE PIGEON BREAST IN CHOCOLATE SAUCE!
DO SOMETHING, KIDS! MY PARCHMENT IS IN PERIL!
WHERE'S MY JUNIOR WOODCHUCK BIRD WHISTLE? HERE WE GO!
FWEEEEEEP!
ALMOST... ALMOST...
?
HEY! THAT'S CHEATING!
ZIP!
COO-COO!
GOOD THINKING, HUEY! BIRDS ARE VERY INTELLIGENT!
COME TO UNCLE SCROOGE, YOU PRECIOUS SQUAB!
WAK!
ANOTHER CRAZY DIAGRAM!
THIS ONE LOOKS MORE COMPLEX THAN THE FIRST!
POST
NO, IT ISN'T! IT'S JUST LIKE THE FIRST! WE'LL FIND A SECOND PAPER
UNDER A CROSS THAT DECORATES
A SPIRE OF THIS CATHEDRAL!

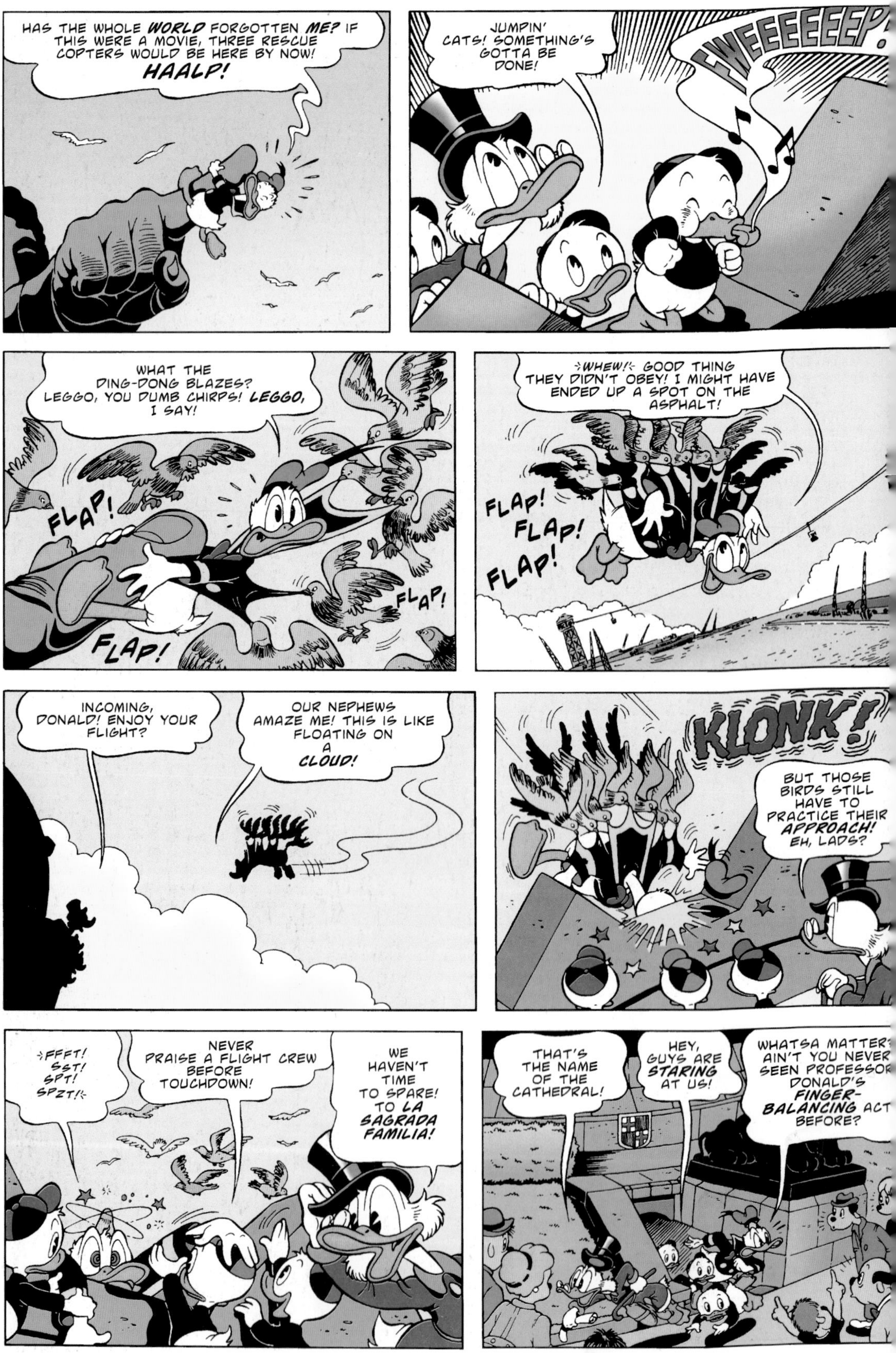
HAS THE WHOLE WORLD FORGOTTEN ME? IF THIS WERE A MOVIE, THREE RESCUE COPTERS WOULD BE HERE BY NOW! HAALP!
JUMPIN' CATS! SOMETHING'S GOTTA BE DONE!
FWEEEEEEP!
WHAT THE DING-DONG BLAZES? LEGGO, YOU DUMB CHIRPS! LEGGO, I SAY!
FLAP!
FLAP!
FLAP!
WHEW! GOOD THING THEY DIDN'T OBEY! I MIGHT HAVE ENDED UP A SPOT ON THE ASPHALT!
FLAP!
FLAP!
FLAP!
INCOMING, DONALD! ENJOY YOUR FLIGHT?
OUR NEPHEWS AMAZE ME! THIS IS LIKE FLOATING ON A CLOUD!
KLONK!
BUT THOSE BIRDS STILL HAVE TO PRACTICE THEIR APPROACH! EH, LADS?
FFFT! SST! SPT! SPZT!
NEVER PRAISE A FLIGHT CREW BEFORE TOUCHDOWN!
WE HAVEN'T TIME TO SPARE! TO LA SAGRADA FAMILIA!
THAT'S THE NAME OF THE CATHEDRAL!
HEY, GUYS ARE STARING AT US!
WHATSA MATTER? AIN'T YOU NEVER SEEN PROFESSOR DONALD'S FINGER-BALANCING ACT BEFORE?

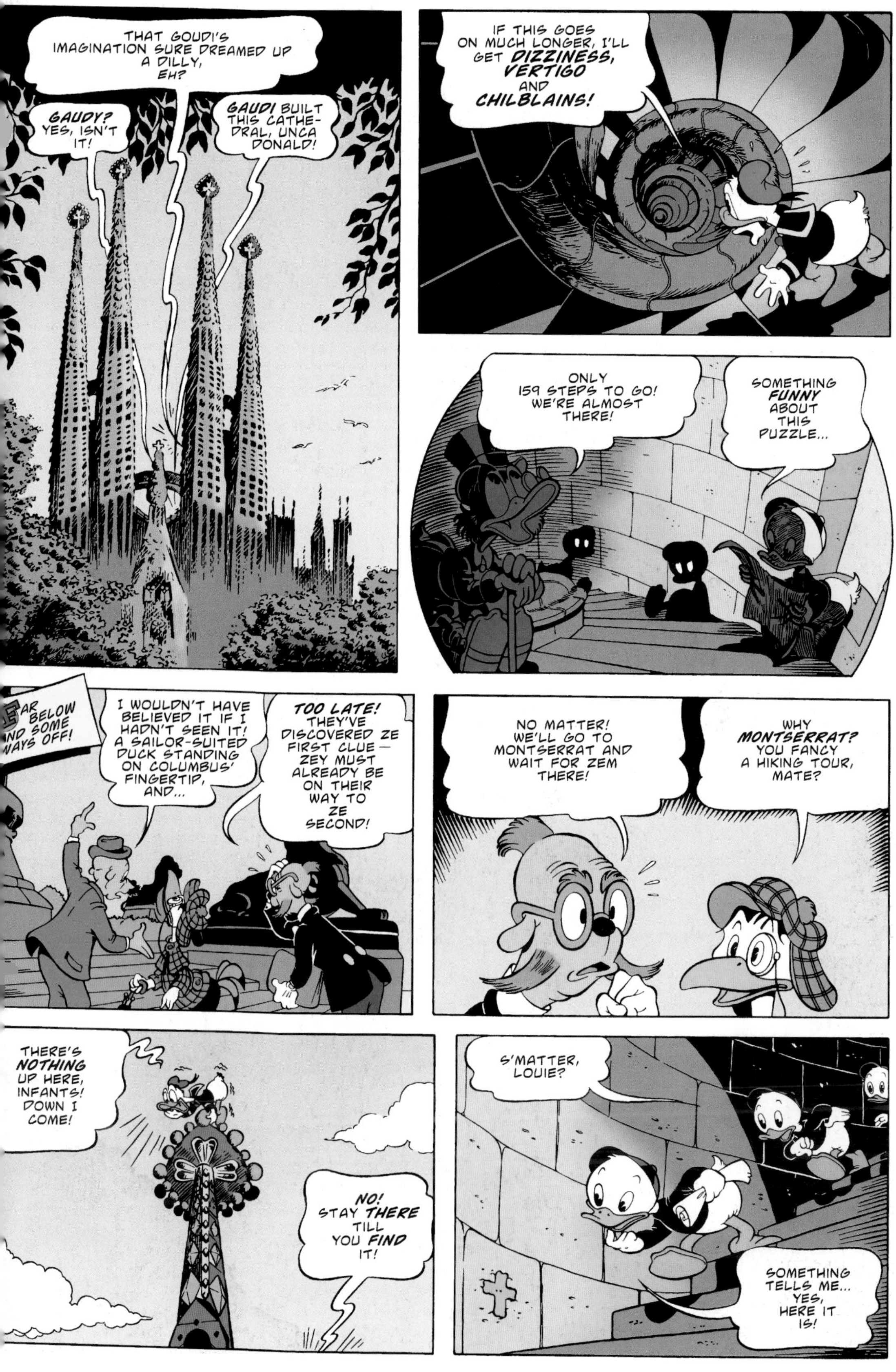
THAT GOUDI'S IMAGINATION SURE DREAMED UP A DILLY, EH?
GAUDY? YES, ISN'T IT!
GAUDI BUILT THIS CATHE-DRAL, UNCA DONALD!
IF THIS GOES ON MUCH LONGER, I'LL GET DIZZINESS, VERTIGO AND CHILBLAINS!
ONLY 159 STEPS TO GO! WE'RE ALMOST THERE!
SOMETHING FUNNY ABOUT THIS PUZZLE...
AR BELOW ND SOME WAYS OFF!
I WOULDN'T HAVE BELIEVED IT IF I HADN'T SEEN IT! A SAILOR-SUITED DUCK STANDING ON COLUMBUS' FINGERTIP, AND...
TOO LATE! THEY'VE DISCOVERED ZE FIRST CLUE — ZEY MUST ALREADY BE ON THEIR WAY TO ZE SECOND!
NO MATTER! WE'LL GO TO MONTSERRAT AND WAIT FOR ZEM THERE!
WHY MONTSERRAT? YOU FANCY A HIKING TOUR, MATE?
THERE'S NOTHING UP HERE, INFANTS! DOWN I COME!
NO! STAY THERE TILL YOU FIND IT!
S'MATTER, LOUIE?
SOMETHING TELLS ME... YES, HERE IT IS!

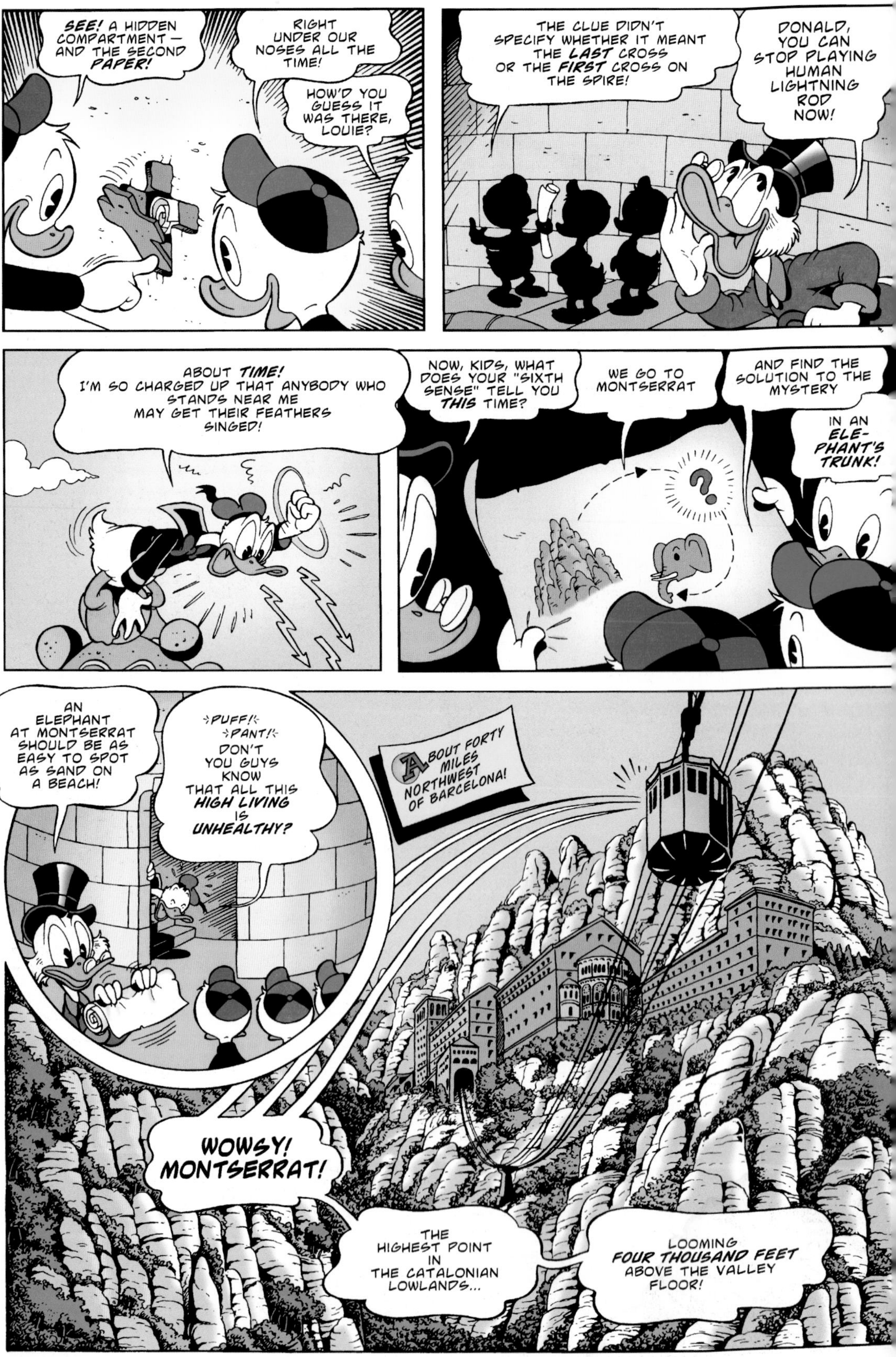
SEE! A HIDDEN COMPARTMENT — AND THE SECOND PAPER!
RIGHT UNDER OUR NOSES ALL THE TIME!
HOW'D YOU GUESS IT WAS THERE, LOUIE?
THE CLUE DIDN'T SPECIFY WHETHER IT MEANT THE LAST CROSS OR THE FIRST CROSS ON THE SPIRE!
DONALD, YOU CAN STOP PLAYING HUMAN LIGHTNING ROD NOW!
ABOUT TIME! I'M SO CHARGED UP THAT ANYBODY WHO STANDS NEAR ME MAY GET THEIR FEATHERS SINGED!
NOW, KIDS, WHAT DOES YOUR "SIXTH SENSE" TELL YOU THIS TIME?
WE GO TO MONTSERRAT
AND FIND THE SOLUTION TO THE MYSTERY
IN AN ELE-PHANT'S TRUNK!
AN ELEPHANT AT MONTSERRAT SHOULD BE AS EASY TO SPOT AS SAND ON A BEACH!
PUFF! PANT! DON'T YOU GUYS KNOW THAT ALL THIS HIGH LIVING IS UNHEALTHY?
ABOUT FORTY MILES NORTHWEST OF BARCELONA!
WOWSY! MONTSERRAT!
THE HIGHEST POINT IN THE CATALONIAN LOWLANDS...
LOOMING FOUR THOUSAND FEET ABOVE THE VALLEY FLOOR!

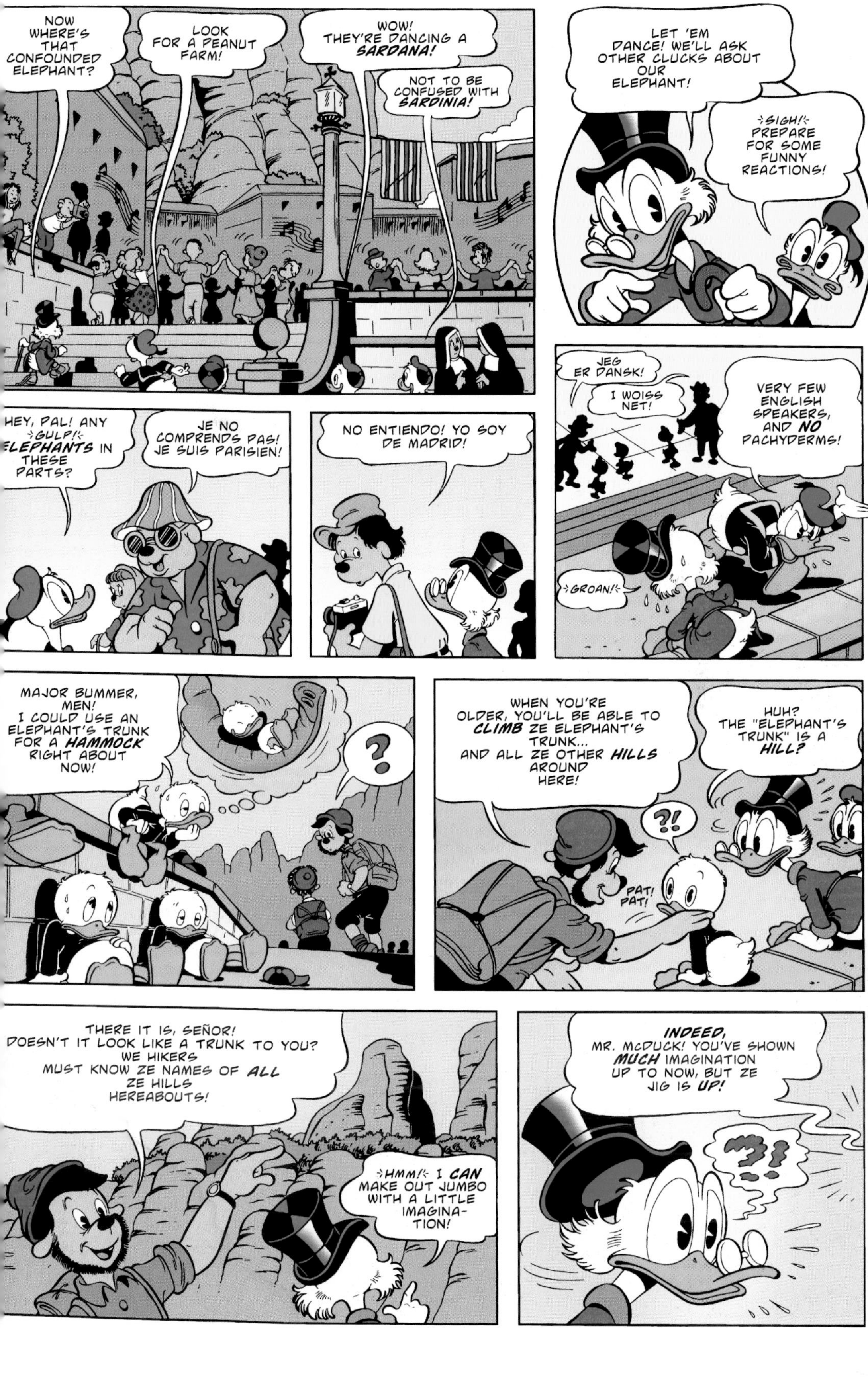

NOW WHERE'S THAT CONFOUNDED ELEPHANT?
LOOK FOR A PEANUT FARM!
WOW! THEY'RE DANCING A **SARDANA!**
NOT TO BE CONFUSED WITH **SARDINIA!**
LET 'EM DANCE! WE'LL ASK OTHER CLUCKS ABOUT OUR ELEPHANT!
SIGH! PREPARE FOR SOME FUNNY REACTIONS!
HEY, PAL! ANY GULP! **ELEPHANTS** IN THESE PARTS?
JE NO COMPRENDS PAS! JE SUIS PARISIEN!
NO ENTIENDO! YO SOY DE MADRID!
JEG ER DANSK!
I WOISS NET!
VERY FEW ENGLISH SPEAKERS, AND **NO** PACHYDERMS!
GROAN!
MAJOR BUMMER, MEN! I COULD USE AN ELEPHANT'S TRUNK FOR A **HAMMOCK** RIGHT ABOUT NOW!
?
WHEN YOU'RE OLDER, YOU'LL BE ABLE TO **CLIMB** ZE ELEPHANT'S TRUNK... AND ALL ZE OTHER **HILLS** AROUND HERE!
HUH? THE "ELEPHANT'S TRUNK" IS A **HILL?**
?!
PAT! PAT!
THERE IT IS, SEÑOR! DOESN'T IT LOOK LIKE A TRUNK TO YOU? WE HIKERS MUST KNOW ZE NAMES OF **ALL** ZE HILLS HEREABOUTS!
HMM! I **CAN** MAKE OUT JUMBO WITH A LITTLE IMAGINA-TION!
INDEED, MR. McDUCK! YOU'VE SHOWN **MUCH** IMAGINATION UP TO NOW, BUT ZE JIG IS **UP!**

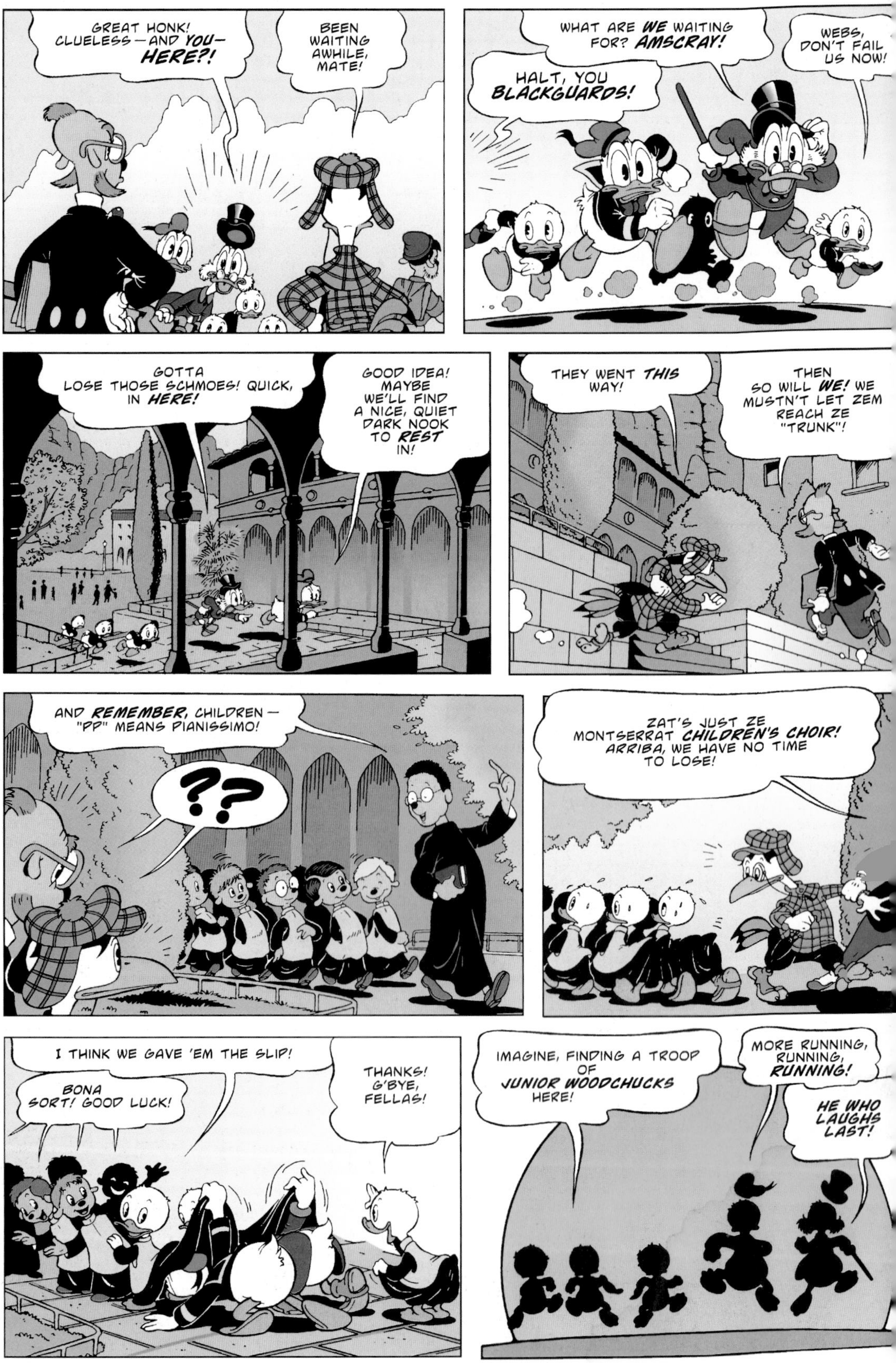
GREAT HONK! CLUELESS—AND YOU—HERE?!
BEEN WAITING AWHILE, MATE!
WHAT ARE WE WAITING FOR? AMSCRAY!
HALT, YOU BLACKGUARDS!
WEBS, DON'T FAIL US NOW!
GOTTA LOSE THOSE SCHMOES! QUICK, IN HERE!
GOOD IDEA! MAYBE WE'LL FIND A NICE, QUIET DARK NOOK TO REST IN!
THEY WENT THIS WAY!
THEN SO WILL WE! WE MUSTN'T LET ZEM REACH ZE "TRUNK"!
AND REMEMBER, CHILDREN— "PP" MEANS PIANISSIMO!
??
ZAT'S JUST ZE MONTSERRAT CHILDREN'S CHOIR! ARRIBA, WE HAVE NO TIME TO LOSE!
I THINK WE GAVE 'EM THE SLIP!
BONA SORT! GOOD LUCK!
THANKS! G'BYE, FELLAS!
IMAGINE, FINDING A TROOP OF JUNIOR WOODCHUCKS HERE!
MORE RUNNING, RUNNING, RUNNING!
HE WHO LAUGHS LAST!

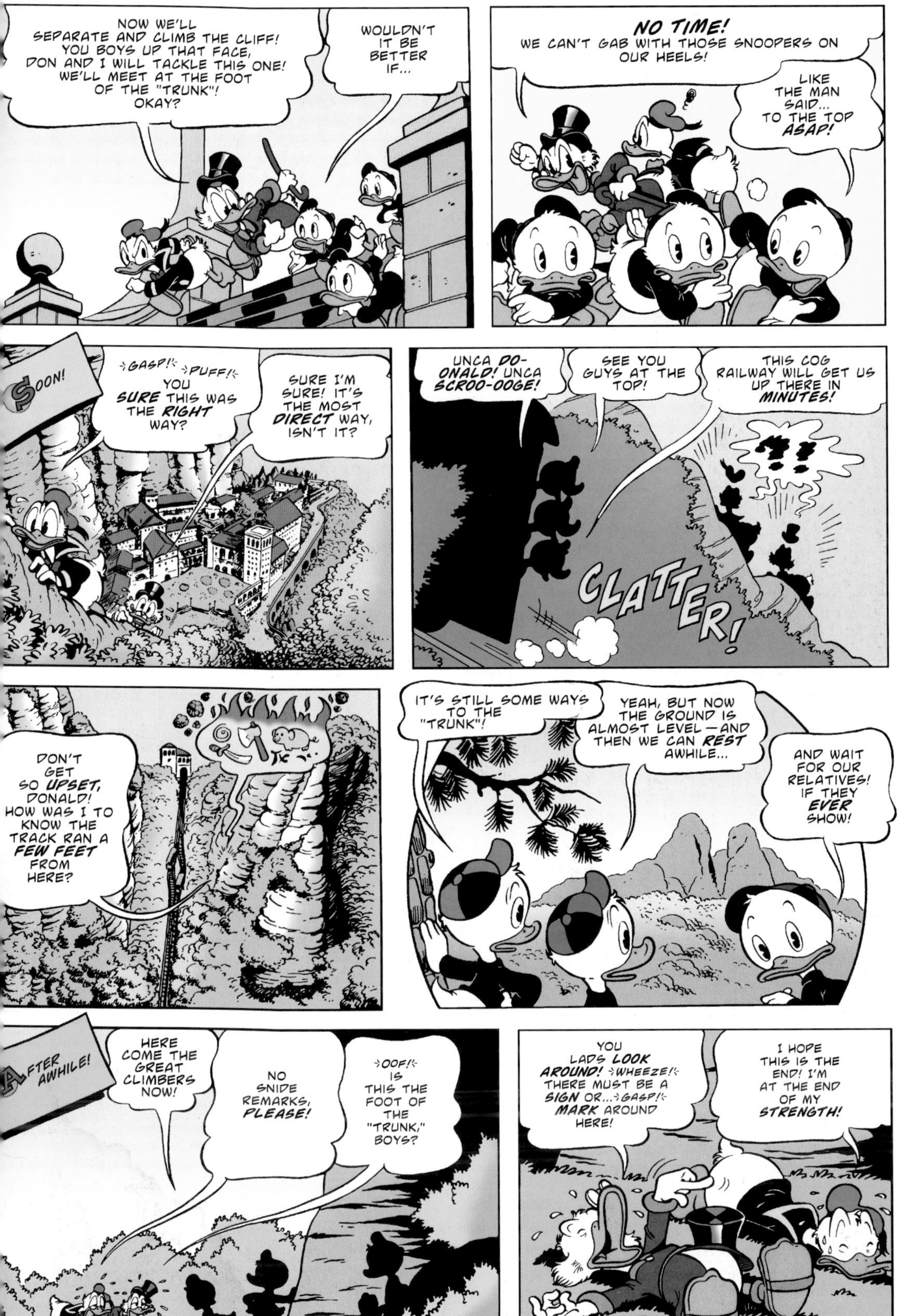
NOW WE'LL SEPARATE AND CLIMB THE CLIFF! YOU BOYS UP THAT FACE, DON AND I WILL TACKLE THIS ONE! WE'LL MEET AT THE FOOT OF THE "TRUNK"! OKAY?
WOULDN'T IT BE BETTER IF...
NO TIME! WE CAN'T GAB WITH THOSE SNOOPERS ON OUR HEELS!
LIKE THE MAN SAID... TO THE TOP ASAP!
SOON!
GASP! PUFF! YOU SURE THIS WAS THE RIGHT WAY?
SURE I'M SURE! IT'S THE MOST DIRECT WAY, ISN'T IT?
UNCA DO-ONALD! UNCA SCROO-OOGE!
SEE YOU GUYS AT THE TOP!
THIS COG RAILWAY WILL GET US UP THERE IN MINUTES!
CLATTER!
DON'T GET SO UPSET, DONALD! HOW WAS I TO KNOW THE TRACK RAN A FEW FEET FROM HERE?
IT'S STILL SOME WAYS TO THE "TRUNK"!
YEAH, BUT NOW THE GROUND IS ALMOST LEVEL—AND THEN WE CAN REST AWHILE...
AND WAIT FOR OUR RELATIVES! IF THEY EVER SHOW!
AFTER AWHILE!
HERE COME THE GREAT CLIMBERS NOW!
NO SNIDE REMARKS, PLEASE!
OOF! IS THIS THE FOOT OF THE "TRUNK," BOYS?
YOU LADS LOOK AROUND! WHEEZE! THERE MUST BE A SIGN OR... GASP! MARK AROUND HERE!
I HOPE THIS IS THE END! I'M AT THE END OF MY STRENGTH!

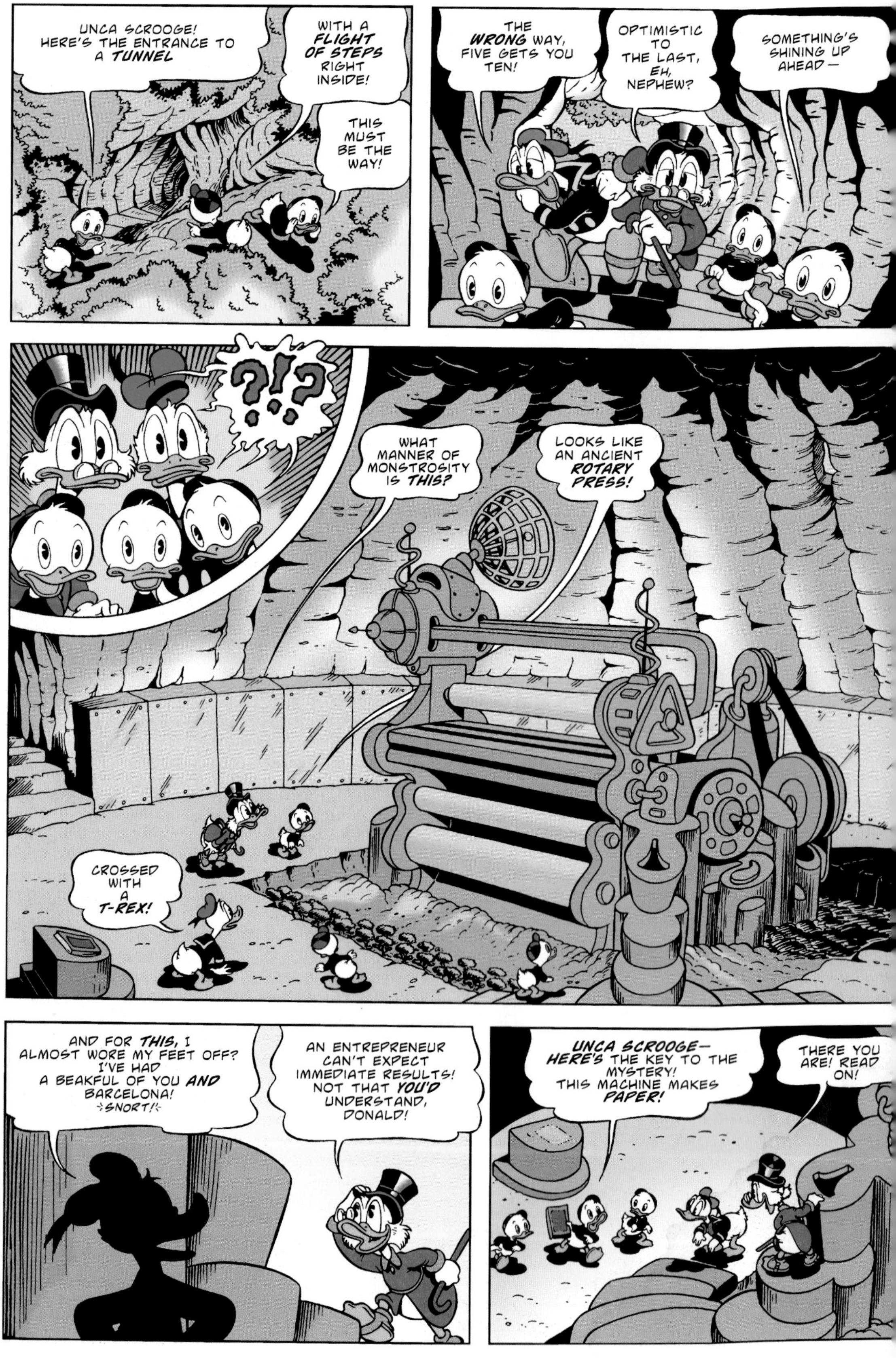
UNCA SCROOGE! HERE'S THE ENTRANCE TO A TUNNEL
WITH A FLIGHT OF STEPS RIGHT INSIDE!
THIS MUST BE THE WAY!
THE WRONG WAY, FIVE GETS YOU TEN!
OPTIMISTIC TO THE LAST, EH, NEPHEW?
SOMETHING'S SHINING UP AHEAD—
?!?
WHAT MANNER OF MONSTROSITY IS THIS?
LOOKS LIKE AN ANCIENT ROTARY PRESS!
CROSSED WITH A T-REX!
AND FOR THIS, I ALMOST WORE MY FEET OFF? I'VE HAD A BEAKFUL OF YOU AND BARCELONA! SNORT!
AN ENTREPRENEUR CAN'T EXPECT IMMEDIATE RESULTS! NOT THAT YOU'D UNDERSTAND, DONALD!
UNCA SCROOGE— HERE'S THE KEY TO THE MYSTERY! THIS MACHINE MAKES PAPER!
THERE YOU ARE! READ ON!

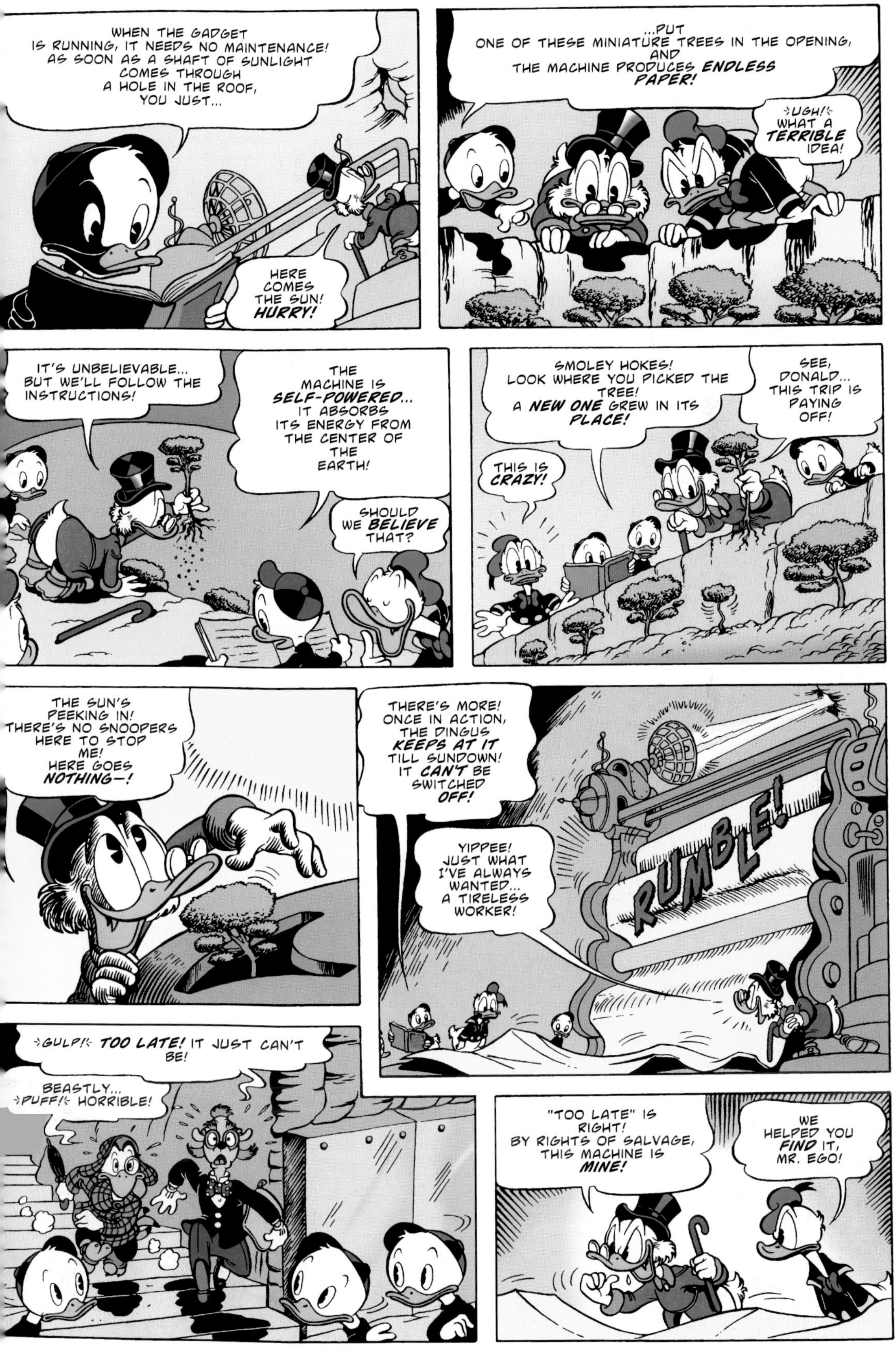
WHEN THE GADGET IS RUNNING, IT NEEDS NO MAINTENANCE! AS SOON AS A SHAFT OF SUNLIGHT COMES THROUGH A HOLE IN THE ROOF, YOU JUST...
HERE COMES THE SUN! HURRY!
...PUT ONE OF THESE MINIATURE TREES IN THE OPENING, AND THE MACHINE PRODUCES ENDLESS PAPER!
UGH! WHAT A TERRIBLE IDEA!
IT'S UNBELIEVABLE... BUT WE'LL FOLLOW THE INSTRUCTIONS!
THE MACHINE IS SELF-POWERED... IT ABSORBS ITS ENERGY FROM THE CENTER OF THE EARTH!
SHOULD WE BELIEVE THAT?
SMOLEY HOKES! LOOK WHERE YOU PICKED THE TREE! A NEW ONE GREW IN ITS PLACE!
SEE, DONALD... THIS TRIP IS PAYING OFF!
THIS IS CRAZY!
THE SUN'S PEEKING IN! THERE'S NO SNOOPERS HERE TO STOP ME! HERE GOES NOTHING—!
THERE'S MORE! ONCE IN ACTION, THE DINGUS KEEPS AT IT TILL SUNDOWN! IT CAN'T BE SWITCHED OFF!
YIPPEE! JUST WHAT I'VE ALWAYS WANTED... A TIRELESS WORKER!
RUMBLE!
GULP! TOO LATE! IT JUST CAN'T BE!
BEASTLY... PUFF! HORRIBLE!
"TOO LATE" IS RIGHT! BY RIGHTS OF SALVAGE, THIS MACHINE IS MINE!
WE HELPED YOU FIND IT, MR. EGO!

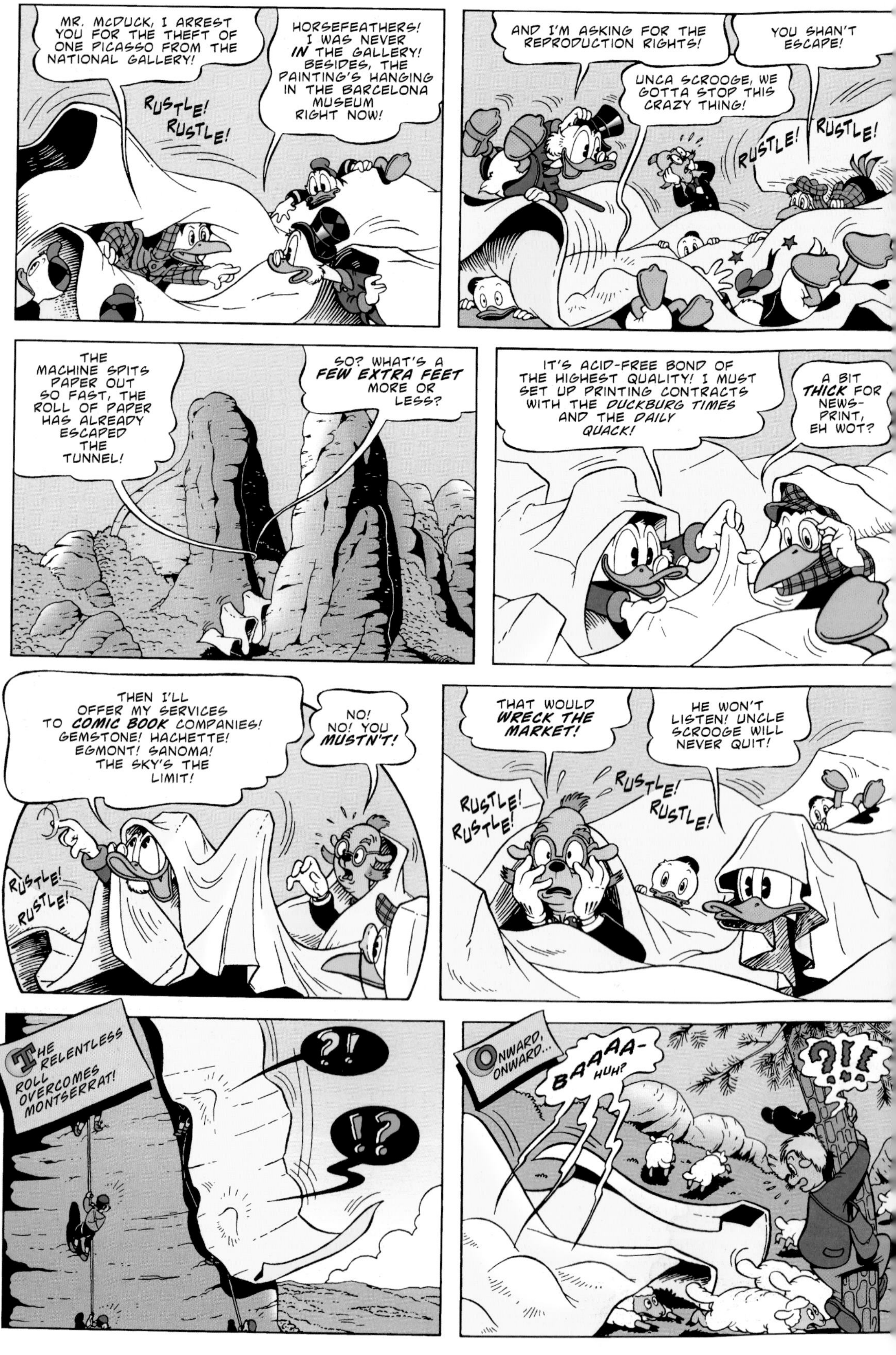
MR. McDUCK, I ARREST YOU FOR THE THEFT OF ONE PICASSO FROM THE NATIONAL GALLERY!
RUSTLE! RUSTLE!
HORSEFEATHERS! I WAS NEVER IN THE GALLERY! BESIDES, THE PAINTING'S HANGING IN THE BARCELONA MUSEUM RIGHT NOW!
AND I'M ASKING FOR THE REPRODUCTION RIGHTS!
YOU SHAN'T ESCAPE!
UNCA SCROOGE, WE GOTTA STOP THIS CRAZY THING!
RUSTLE! RUSTLE!
THE MACHINE SPITS PAPER OUT SO FAST, THE ROLL OF PAPER HAS ALREADY ESCAPED THE TUNNEL!
SO? WHAT'S A FEW EXTRA FEET MORE OR LESS?
IT'S ACID-FREE BOND OF THE HIGHEST QUALITY! I MUST SET UP PRINTING CONTRACTS WITH THE DUCKBURG TIMES AND THE DAILY QUACK!
A BIT THICK FOR NEWS-PRINT, EH WOT?
THEN I'LL OFFER MY SERVICES TO COMIC BOOK COMPANIES! GEMSTONE! HACHETTE! EGMONT! SANOMA! THE SKY'S THE LIMIT!
NO! NO! YOU MUSTN'T!
RUSTLE! RUSTLE!
THAT WOULD WRECK THE MARKET!
HE WON'T LISTEN! UNCLE SCROOGE WILL NEVER QUIT!
RUSTLE! RUSTLE!
RUSTLE! RUSTLE!
THE RELENTLESS ROLL OVERCOMES MONTSERRAT!
?!
!?
ONWARD, ONWARD...
BAAAA-HUH?
?!!

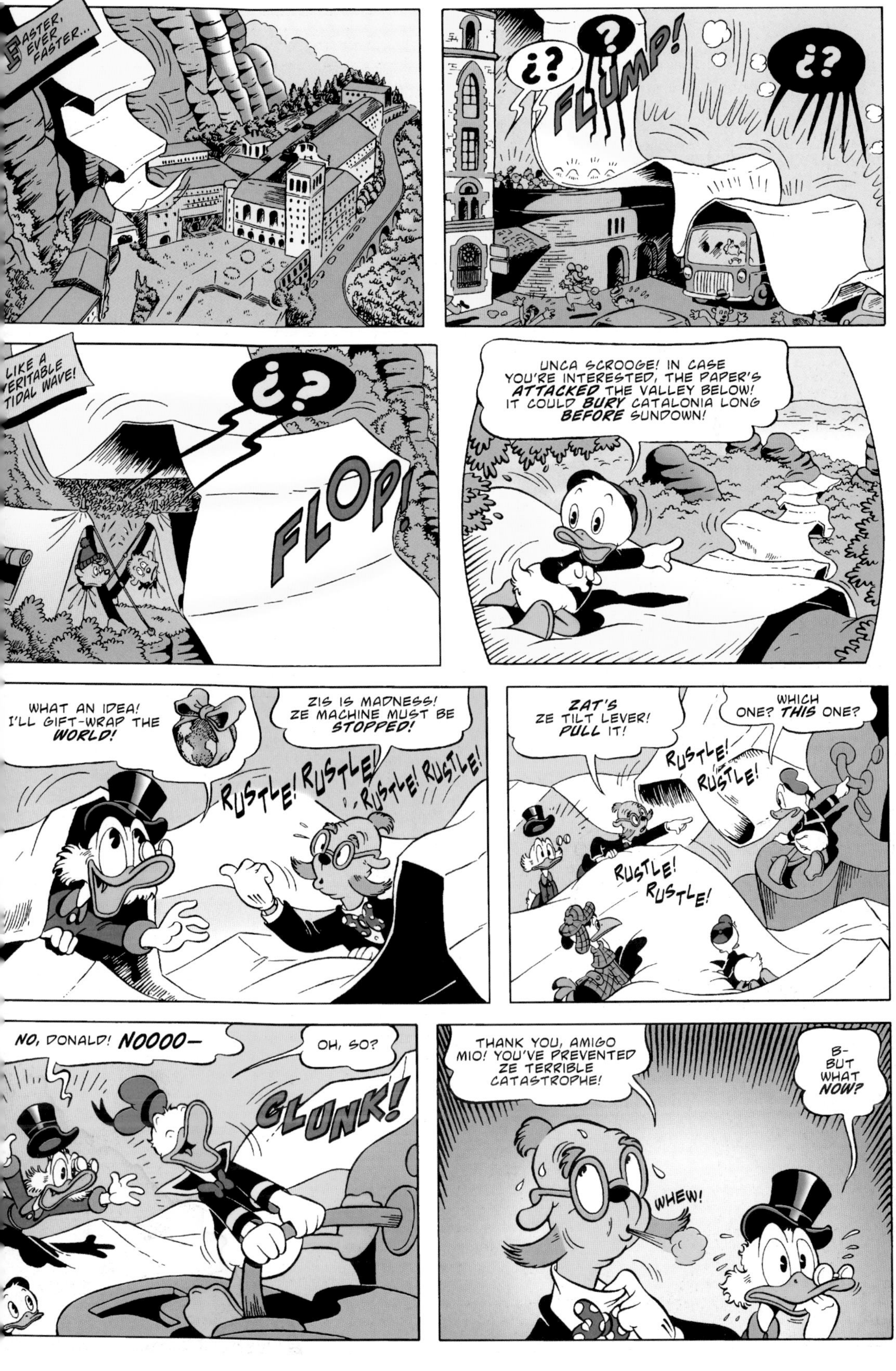
FASTER, EVER FASTER...
¿?
FLUMP!
?
¿?
LIKE A VERITABLE TIDAL WAVE!
¿?
FLOP!
UNCA SCROOGE! IN CASE YOU'RE INTERESTED, THE PAPER'S ATTACKED THE VALLEY BELOW! IT COULD BURY CATALONIA LONG BEFORE SUNDOWN!
WHAT AN IDEA! I'LL GIFT-WRAP THE WORLD!
ZIS IS MADNESS! ZE MACHINE MUST BE STOPPED!
RUSTLE! RUSTLE! RUSTLE! RUSTLE!
ZAT'S ZE TILT LEVER! PULL IT!
WHICH ONE? THIS ONE?
RUSTLE! RUSTLE!
RUSTLE! RUSTLE!
NO, DONALD! NOOOO—
OH, SO?
CLUNK!
THANK YOU, AMIGO MIO! YOU'VE PREVENTED ZE TERRIBLE CATASTROPHE!
B-BUT WHAT NOW?
WHEW!

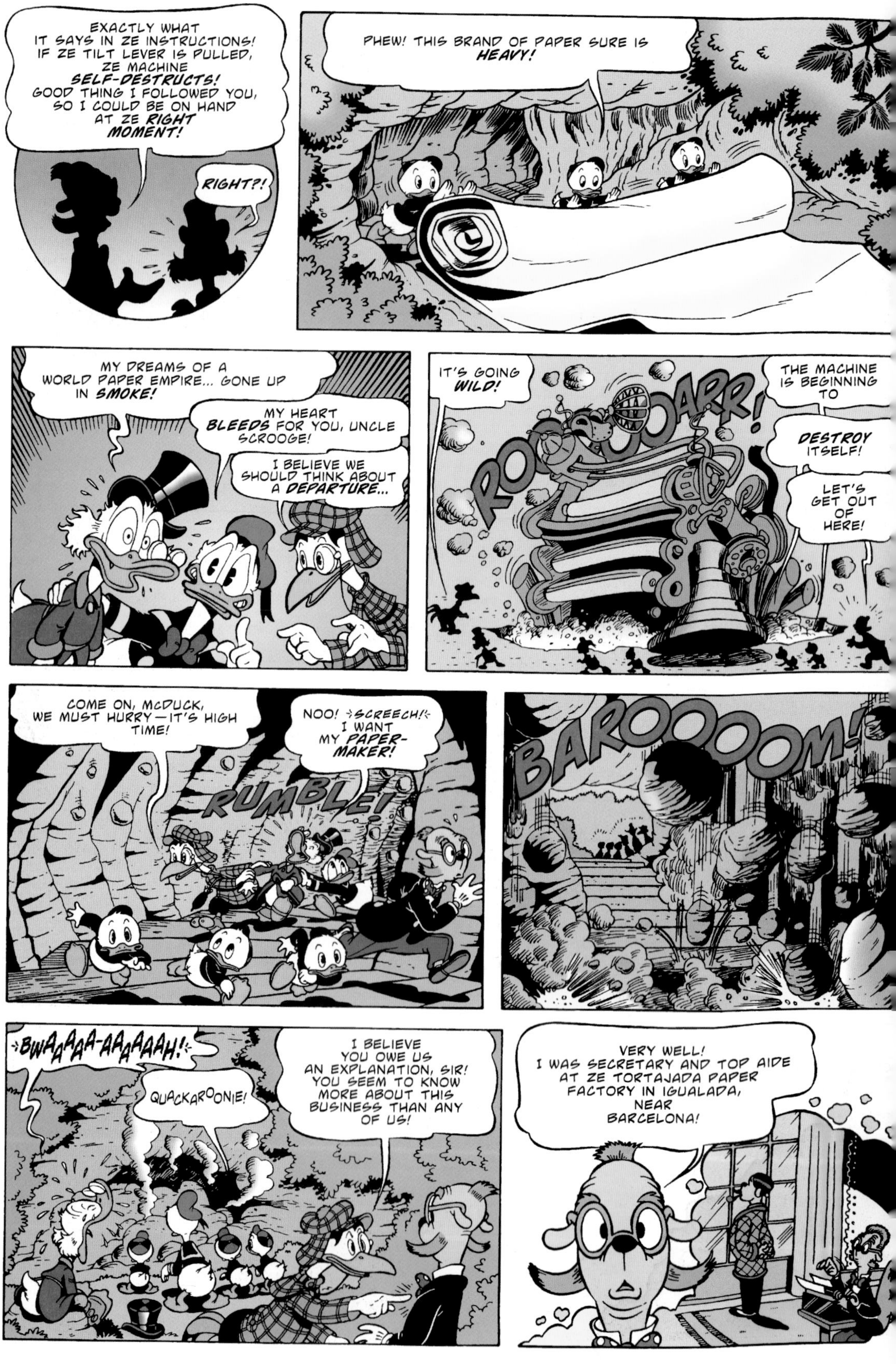
EXACTLY WHAT IT SAYS IN ZE INSTRUCTIONS! IF ZE TILT LEVER IS PULLED, ZE MACHINE SELF-DESTRUCTS! GOOD THING I FOLLOWED YOU, SO I COULD BE ON HAND AT ZE RIGHT MOMENT!
RIGHT?!
PHEW! THIS BRAND OF PAPER SURE IS HEAVY!
MY DREAMS OF A WORLD PAPER EMPIRE... GONE UP IN SMOKE!
MY HEART BLEEDS FOR YOU, UNCLE SCROOGE!
I BELIEVE WE SHOULD THINK ABOUT A DEPARTURE...
IT'S GOING WILD!
ROOOOARR!
THE MACHINE IS BEGINNING TO
DESTROY ITSELF!
LET'S GET OUT OF HERE!
COME ON, McDUCK, WE MUST HURRY—IT'S HIGH TIME!
NOO! ‹SCREECH!› I WANT MY PAPER-MAKER!
RUMBLE!
BAROOOOOM!
BWAAAAA-AAAAAAH!
QUACKAROONIE!
I BELIEVE YOU OWE US AN EXPLANATION, SIR! YOU SEEM TO KNOW MORE ABOUT THIS BUSINESS THAN ANY OF US!
VERY WELL! I WAS SECRETARY AND TOP AIDE AT ZE TORTAJADA PAPER FACTORY IN IGUALADA, NEAR BARCELONA!

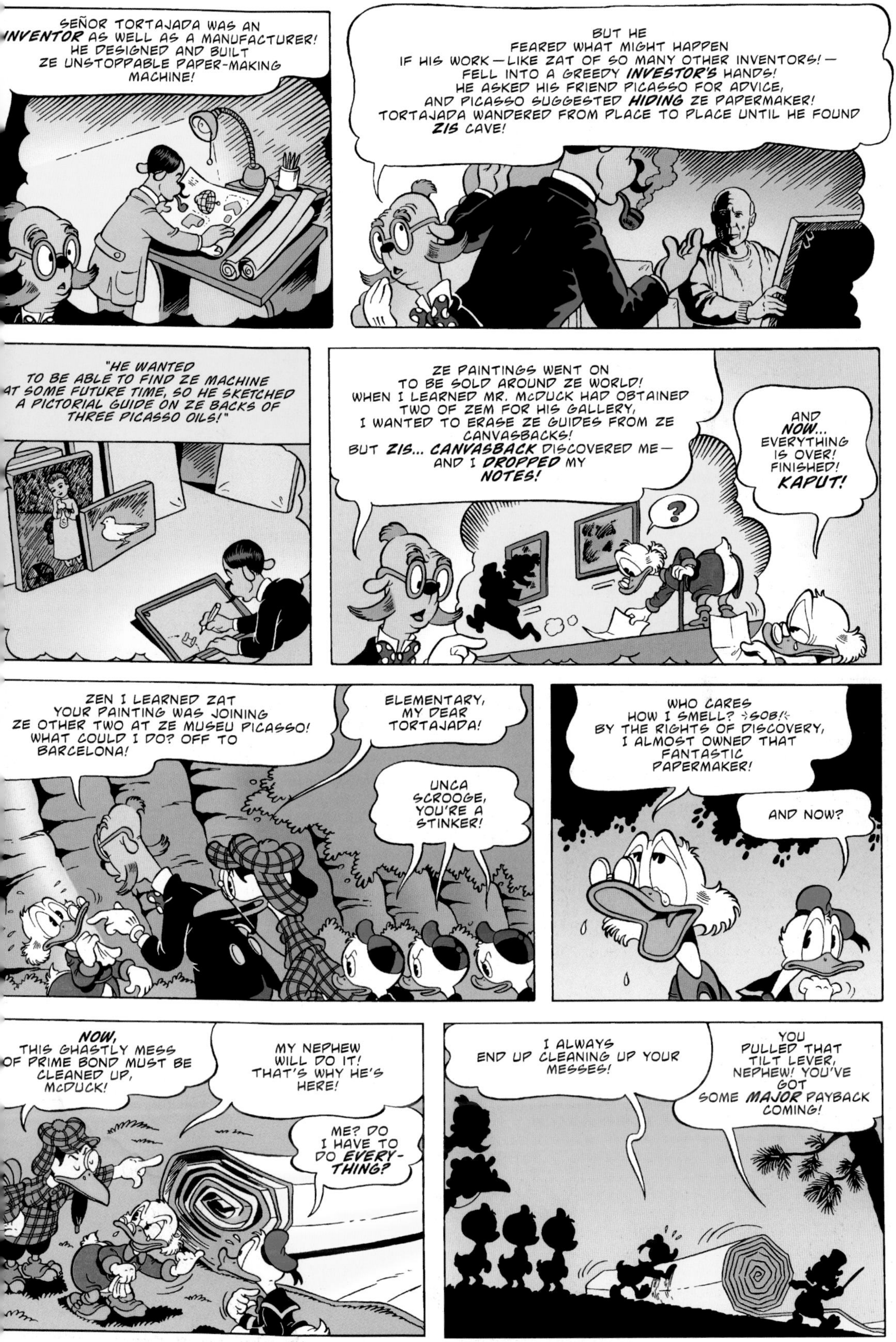
SEÑOR TORTAJADA WAS AN INVENTOR AS WELL AS A MANUFACTURER! HE DESIGNED AND BUILT ZE UNSTOPPABLE PAPER-MAKING MACHINE!
BUT HE FEARED WHAT MIGHT HAPPEN IF HIS WORK—LIKE ZAT OF SO MANY OTHER INVENTORS!—FELL INTO A GREEDY INVESTOR'S HANDS! HE ASKED HIS FRIEND PICASSO FOR ADVICE, AND PICASSO SUGGESTED HIDING ZE PAPERMAKER! TORTAJADA WANDERED FROM PLACE TO PLACE UNTIL HE FOUND ZIS CAVE!
"HE WANTED TO BE ABLE TO FIND ZE MACHINE AT SOME FUTURE TIME, SO HE SKETCHED A PICTORIAL GUIDE ON ZE BACKS OF THREE PICASSO OILS!"
ZE PAINTINGS WENT ON TO BE SOLD AROUND ZE WORLD! WHEN I LEARNED MR. McDUCK HAD OBTAINED TWO OF ZEM FOR HIS GALLERY, I WANTED TO ERASE ZE GUIDES FROM ZE CANVASBACKS! BUT ZIS... CANVASBACK DISCOVERED ME—AND I DROPPED MY NOTES!
?
AND NOW... EVERYTHING IS OVER! FINISHED! KAPUT!
ZEN I LEARNED ZAT YOUR PAINTING WAS JOINING ZE OTHER TWO AT ZE MUSEU PICASSO! WHAT COULD I DO? OFF TO BARCELONA!
ELEMENTARY, MY DEAR TORTAJADA!
UNCA SCROOGE, YOU'RE A STINKER!
WHO CARES HOW I SMELL? SOB! BY THE RIGHTS OF DISCOVERY, I ALMOST OWNED THAT FANTASTIC PAPERMAKER!
AND NOW?
NOW, THIS GHASTLY MESS OF PRIME BOND MUST BE CLEANED UP, McDUCK!
MY NEPHEW WILL DO IT! THAT'S WHY HE'S HERE!
ME? DO I HAVE TO DO EVERYTHING?
I ALWAYS END UP CLEANING UP YOUR MESSES!
YOU PULLED THAT TILT LEVER, NEPHEW! YOU'VE GOT SOME MAJOR PAYBACK COMING!

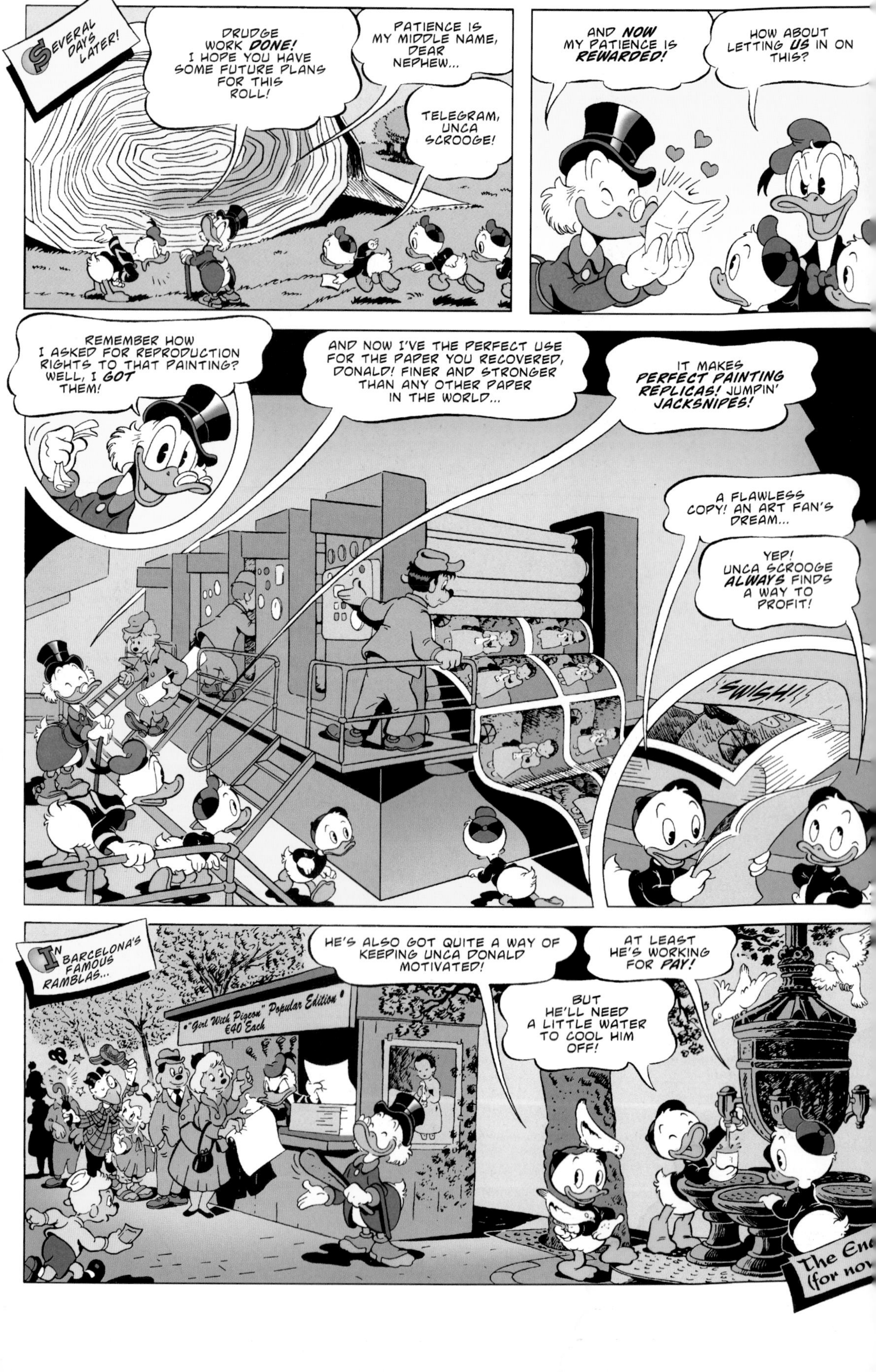
SEVERAL DAYS LATER!
DRUDGE WORK DONE! I HOPE YOU HAVE SOME FUTURE PLANS FOR THIS ROLL!
PATIENCE IS MY MIDDLE NAME, DEAR NEPHEW...
TELEGRAM, UNCA SCROOGE!
AND NOW MY PATIENCE IS REWARDED!
HOW ABOUT LETTING US IN ON THIS?
REMEMBER HOW I ASKED FOR REPRODUCTION RIGHTS TO THAT PAINTING? WELL, I GOT THEM!
AND NOW I'VE THE PERFECT USE FOR THE PAPER YOU RECOVERED, DONALD! FINER AND STRONGER THAN ANY OTHER PAPER IN THE WORLD...
IT MAKES PERFECT PAINTING REPLICAS! JUMPIN' JACKSNIPES!
A FLAWLESS COPY! AN ART FAN'S DREAM...
YEP! UNCA SCROOGE ALWAYS FINDS A WAY TO PROFIT!
SWISH!
IN BARCELONA'S FAMOUS RAMBLAS...
"Girl With Pigeon" Popular Edition €40 Each
HE'S ALSO GOT QUITE A WAY OF KEEPING UNCA DONALD MOTIVATED!
AT LEAST HE'S WORKING FOR PAY!
BUT HE'LL NEED A LITTLE WATER TO COOL HIM OFF!
The End (for now

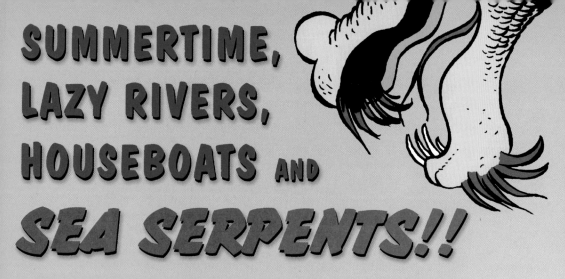

SUMMERTIME, LAZY RIVERS, HOUSEBOATS AND SEA SERPENTS!!

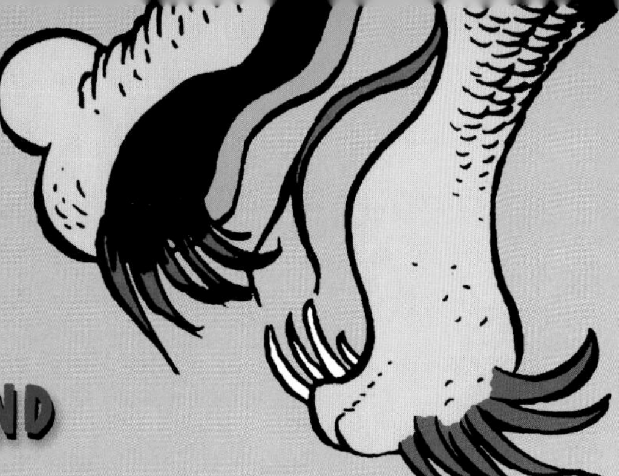

When Donald and his nephews set sail on their new houseboat for fun and adventure, their voyage is riddled with mishaps, blunders, and foul-ups... would you expect anything less from Donald? But something beyond their wildest imaginations lurks beneath the lazy waters of the Ohio River, and as usual, it's up to the nephews to crack the case!

Ride along with the ducks in Carl Barks' classic adventure, "The Terror of the River!!" in *Vacation Parade 3,* Gemstone Publishing's fun-filled collection of summertime favorites! Available at your local comic shop in May, 2006.

This year's Summer spectacular also features the wrap-around cover from the original *Vacation Parade* 3, professionally restored by Rick Keene, as well as:

- A Don Rosa pin-up page of "Terror of the River!!"
- Mickey Mouse in "Sandgate," by Noel Van Horn
- Donald and Fethry in "The Fall Guy" by Dick Kinney and Al Hubbard
- "Goofy Gives His All" by Sarah Kinney and Rodriquez
- Pluto in "The-Not-So-Still Life," by Paul Murry (from *Walt Disney's Comics and Stories* 186)
- Li'l Bad Wolf in "Fooling the Fairy," by Gil Turner (from *Walt Disney's Comics and Stories* 102)

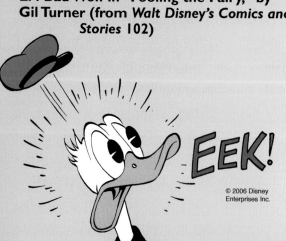

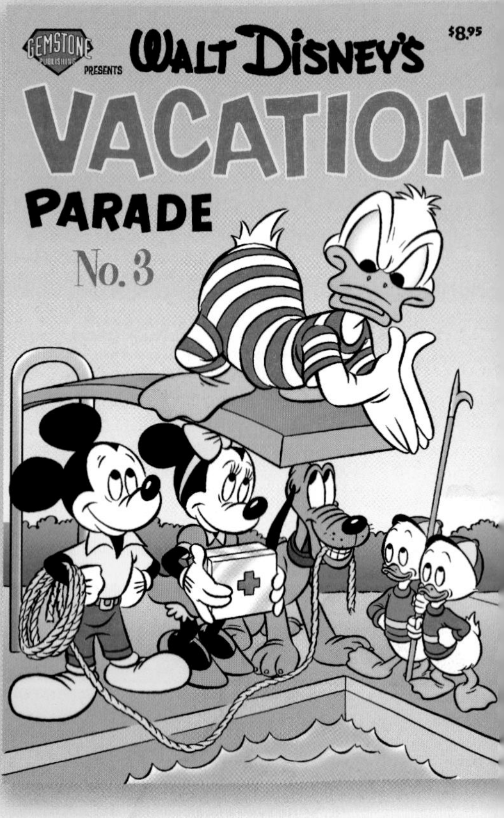
GEMSTONE PUBLISHING
PRESENTS
WALT DISNEY'S
$8.95
VACATION
PARADE
No. 3

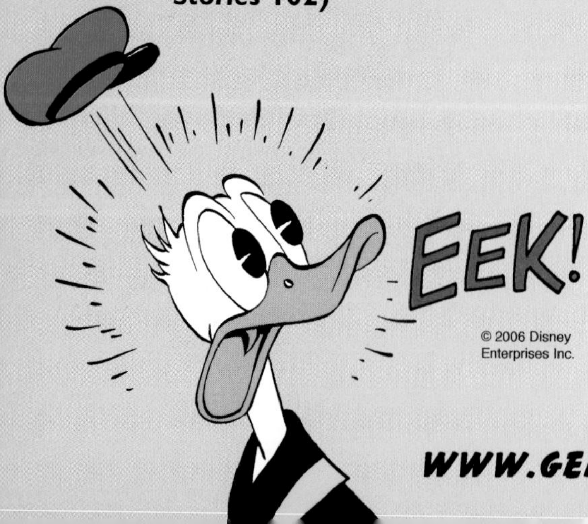
EEK!

WWW.GEMSTONEPUB.COM/DISNEY

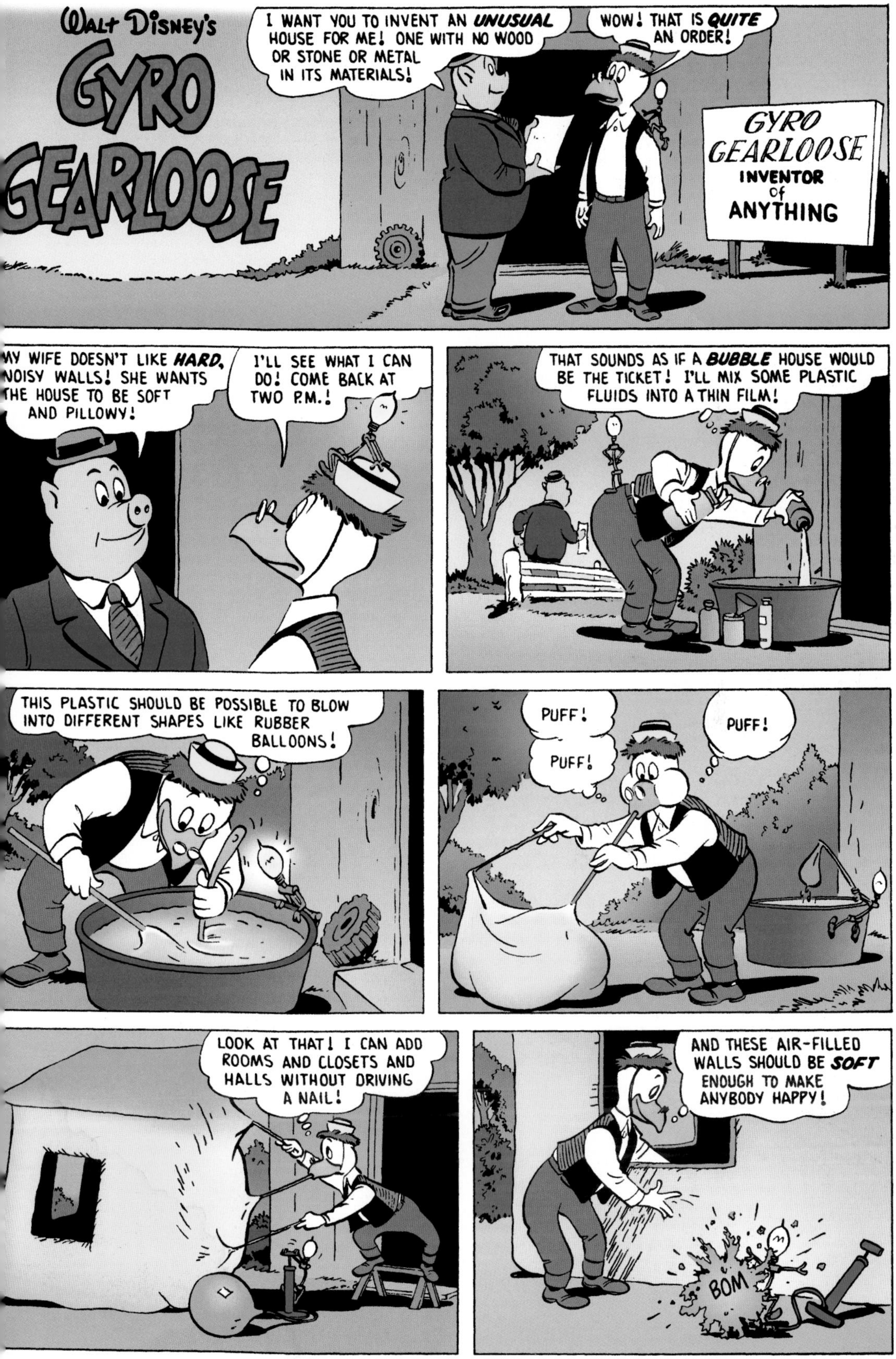
Walt Disney's
GYRO GEARLOOSE
I WANT YOU TO INVENT AN UNUSUAL HOUSE FOR ME! ONE WITH NO WOOD OR STONE OR METAL IN ITS MATERIALS!
WOW! THAT IS QUITE AN ORDER!
GYRO GEARLOOSE INVENTOR Of ANYTHING
MY WIFE DOESN'T LIKE HARD, NOISY WALLS! SHE WANTS THE HOUSE TO BE SOFT AND PILLOWY!
I'LL SEE WHAT I CAN DO! COME BACK AT TWO P.M.!
THAT SOUNDS AS IF A BUBBLE HOUSE WOULD BE THE TICKET! I'LL MIX SOME PLASTIC FLUIDS INTO A THIN FILM!
THIS PLASTIC SHOULD BE POSSIBLE TO BLOW INTO DIFFERENT SHAPES LIKE RUBBER BALLOONS!
PUFF!
PUFF!
PUFF!
LOOK AT THAT! I CAN ADD ROOMS AND CLOSETS AND HALLS WITHOUT DRIVING A NAIL!
AND THESE AIR-FILLED WALLS SHOULD BE SOFT ENOUGH TO MAKE ANYBODY HAPPY!
BOM

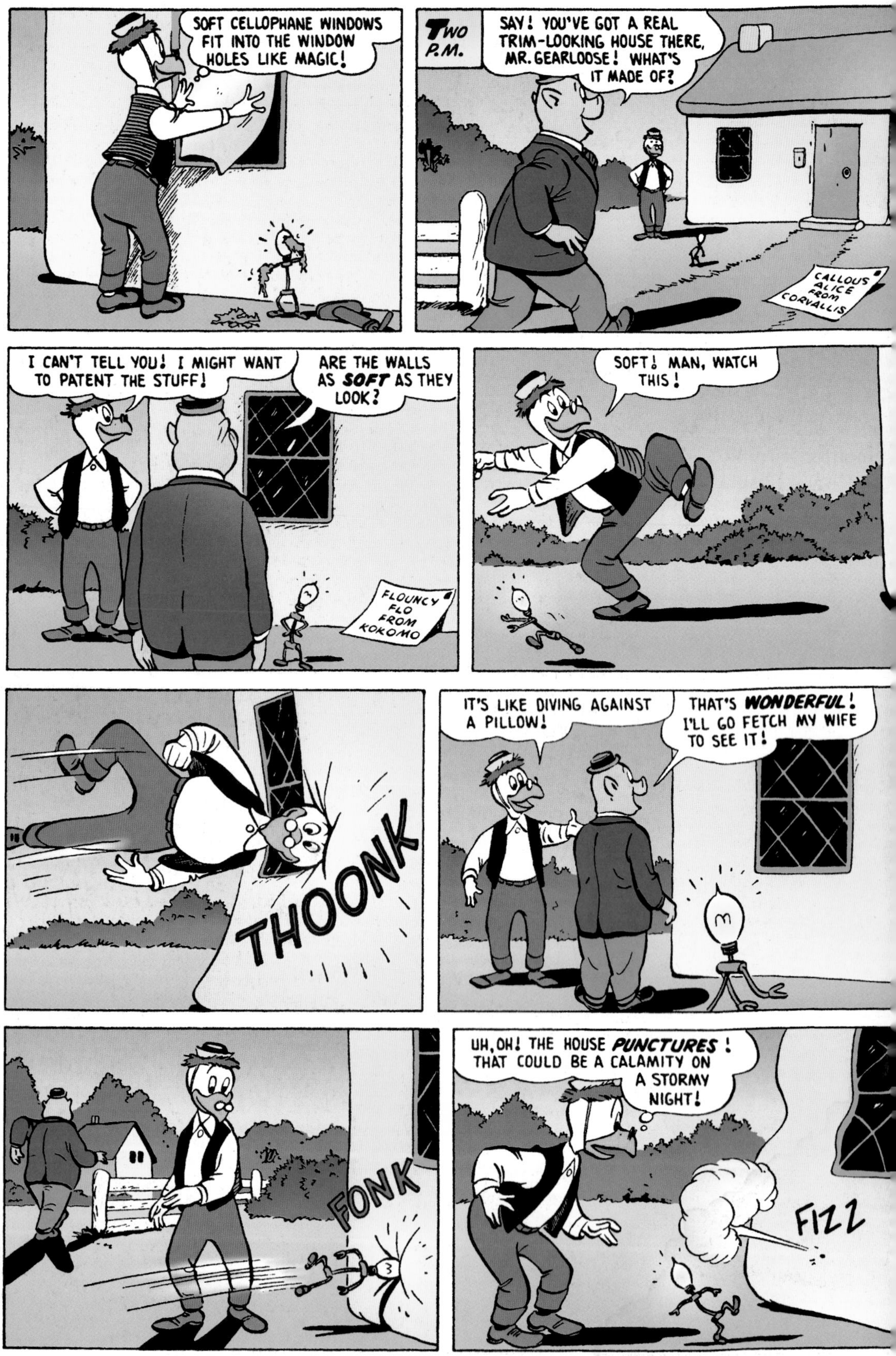
SOFT CELLOPHANE WINDOWS FIT INTO THE WINDOW HOLES LIKE MAGIC!
TWO P.M.
SAY! YOU'VE GOT A REAL TRIM-LOOKING HOUSE THERE, MR. GEARLOOSE! WHAT'S IT MADE OF?
CALLOUS ALICE FROM CORVALLIS
I CAN'T TELL YOU! I MIGHT WANT TO PATENT THE STUFF!
ARE THE WALLS AS SOFT AS THEY LOOK?
FLOUNCY FLO FROM KOKOMO
SOFT! MAN, WATCH THIS!
THOONK
IT'S LIKE DIVING AGAINST A PILLOW!
THAT'S WONDERFUL! I'LL GO FETCH MY WIFE TO SEE IT!
FONK
UH, OH! THE HOUSE PUNCTURES! THAT COULD BE A CALAMITY ON A STORMY NIGHT!
FIZZ

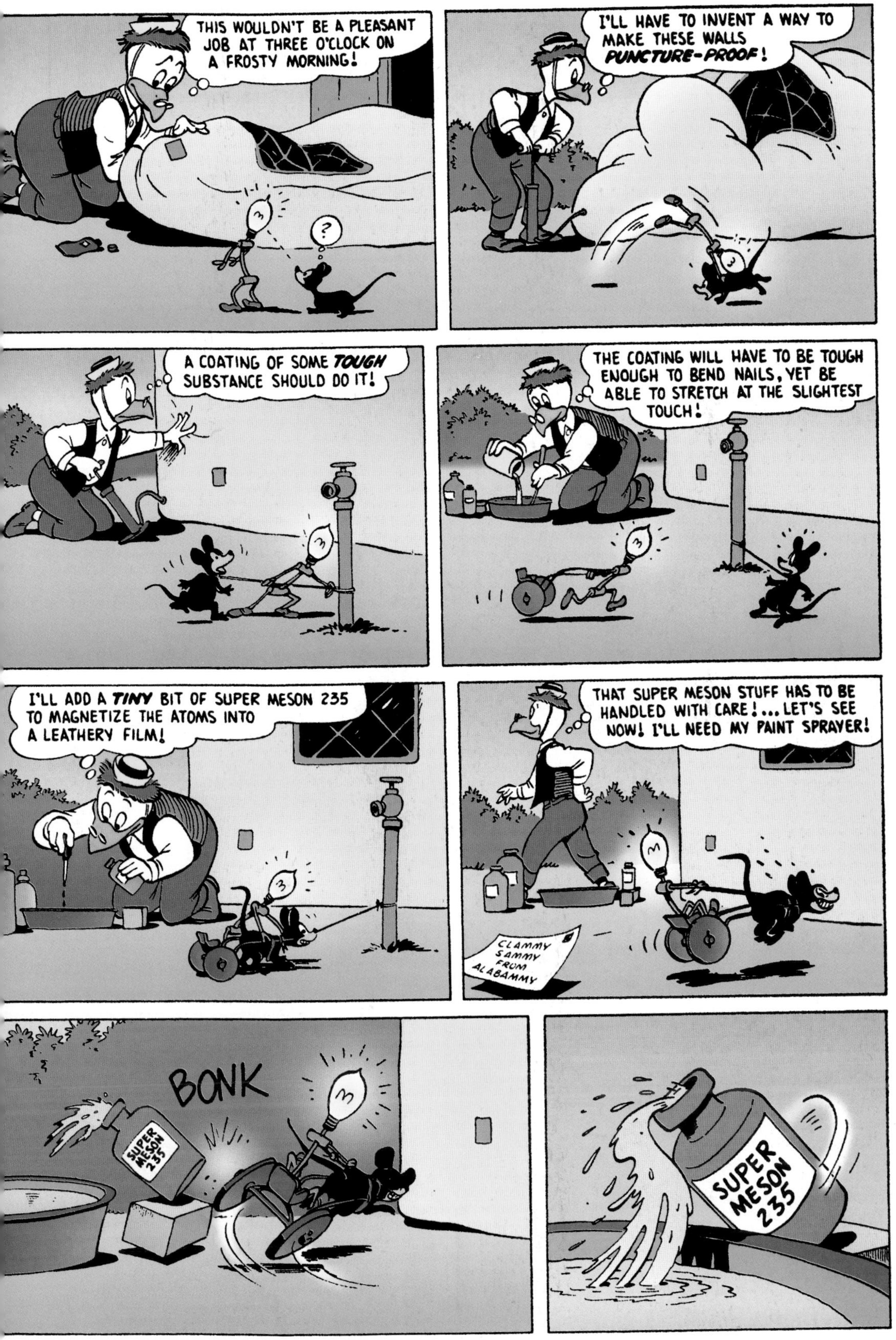
THIS WOULDN'T BE A PLEASANT JOB AT THREE O'CLOCK ON A FROSTY MORNING!
I'LL HAVE TO INVENT A WAY TO MAKE THESE WALLS PUNCTURE-PROOF!
A COATING OF SOME TOUGH SUBSTANCE SHOULD DO IT!
THE COATING WILL HAVE TO BE TOUGH ENOUGH TO BEND NAILS, YET BE ABLE TO STRETCH AT THE SLIGHTEST TOUCH!
I'LL ADD A TINY BIT OF SUPER MESON 235 TO MAGNETIZE THE ATOMS INTO A LEATHERY FILM!
THAT SUPER MESON STUFF HAS TO BE HANDLED WITH CARE!... LET'S SEE NOW! I'LL NEED MY PAINT SPRAYER!
CLAMMY SAMMY FROM ALABAMMY
BONK
SUPER MESON 235
SUPER MESON 235

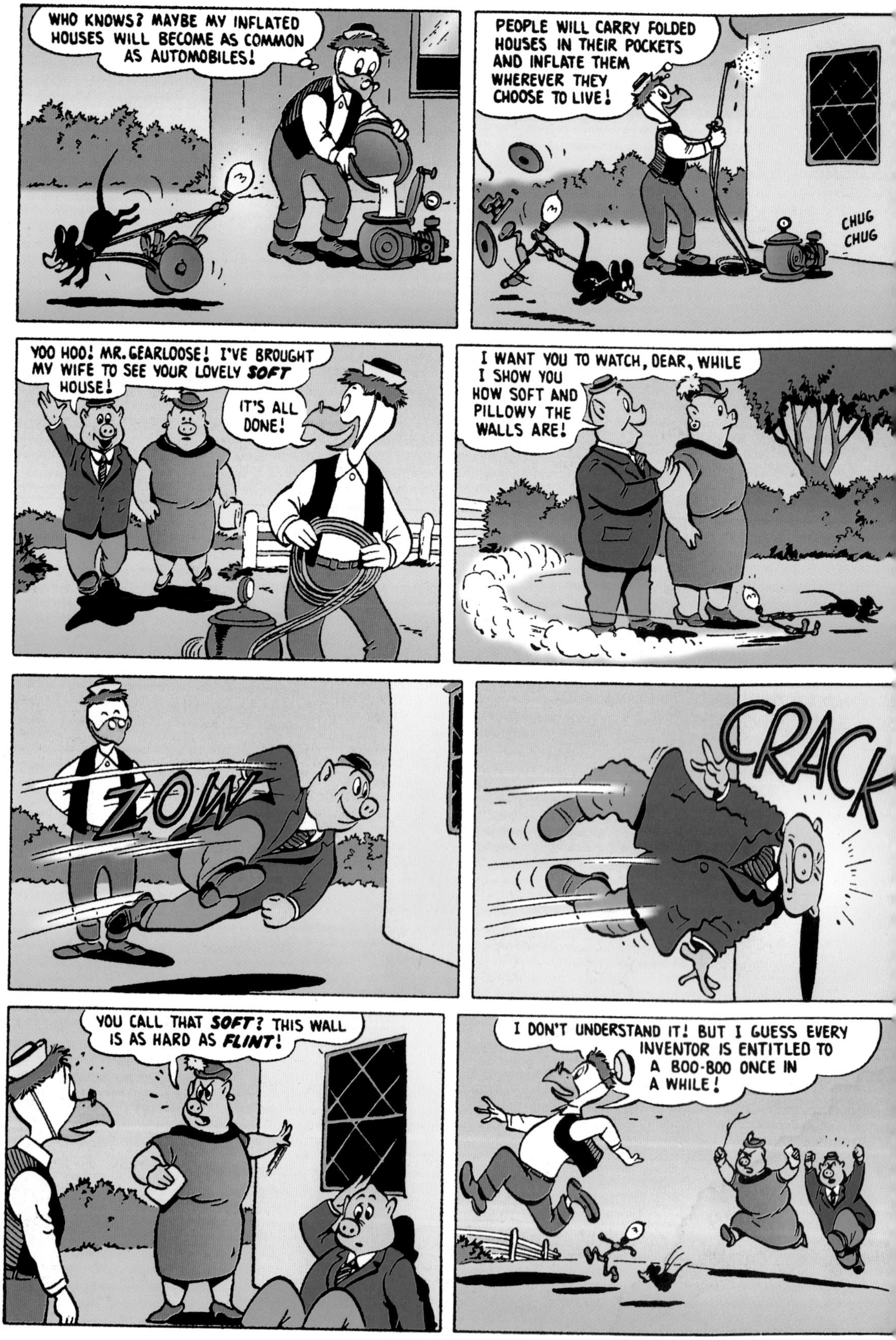
WHO KNOWS? MAYBE MY INFLATED HOUSES WILL BECOME AS COMMON AS AUTOMOBILES!
PEOPLE WILL CARRY FOLDED HOUSES IN THEIR POCKETS AND INFLATE THEM WHEREVER THEY CHOOSE TO LIVE!
CHUG CHUG
YOO HOO! MR. GEARLOOSE! I'VE BROUGHT MY WIFE TO SEE YOUR LOVELY SOFT HOUSE!
IT'S ALL DONE!
I WANT YOU TO WATCH, DEAR, WHILE I SHOW YOU HOW SOFT AND PILLOWY THE WALLS ARE!
ZOW
CRACK
YOU CALL THAT SOFT? THIS WALL IS AS HARD AS FLINT!
I DON'T UNDERSTAND IT! BUT I GUESS EVERY INVENTOR IS ENTITLED TO A BOO-BOO ONCE IN A WHILE!

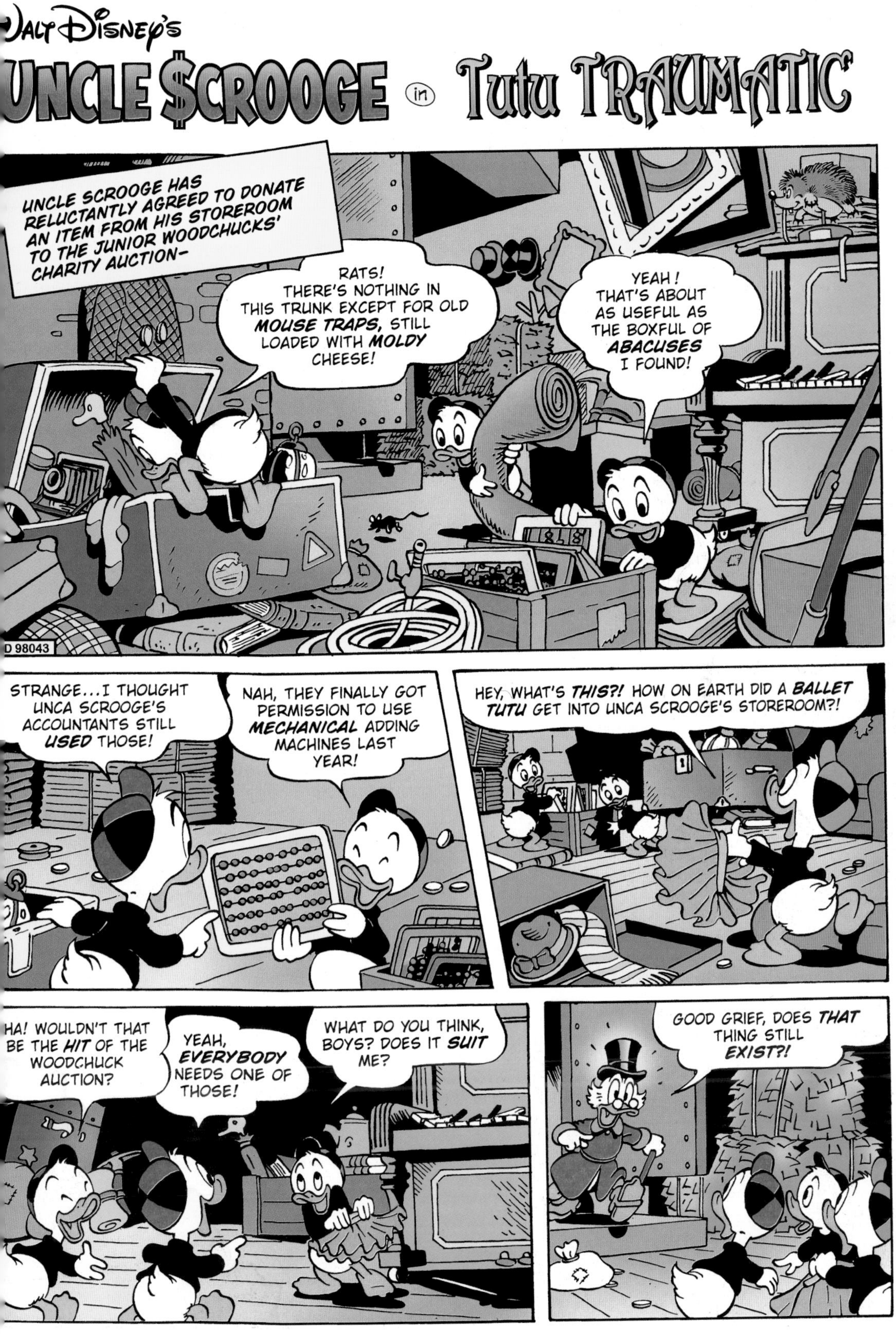
WALT DISNEY'S
UNCLE $CROOGE in Tutu TRAUMATIC
UNCLE SCROOGE HAS RELUCTANTLY AGREED TO DONATE AN ITEM FROM HIS STOREROOM TO THE JUNIOR WOODCHUCKS' CHARITY AUCTION–
RATS! THERE'S NOTHING IN THIS TRUNK EXCEPT FOR OLD MOUSE TRAPS, STILL LOADED WITH MOLDY CHEESE!
YEAH! THAT'S ABOUT AS USEFUL AS THE BOXFUL OF ABACUSES I FOUND!
D 98043
STRANGE...I THOUGHT UNCA SCROOGE'S ACCOUNTANTS STILL USED THOSE!
NAH, THEY FINALLY GOT PERMISSION TO USE MECHANICAL ADDING MACHINES LAST YEAR!
HEY, WHAT'S THIS?! HOW ON EARTH DID A BALLET TUTU GET INTO UNCA SCROOGE'S STOREROOM?!
HA! WOULDN'T THAT BE THE HIT OF THE WOODCHUCK AUCTION?
YEAH, EVERYBODY NEEDS ONE OF THOSE!
WHAT DO YOU THINK, BOYS? DOES IT SUIT ME?
GOOD GRIEF, DOES THAT THING STILL EXIST?!

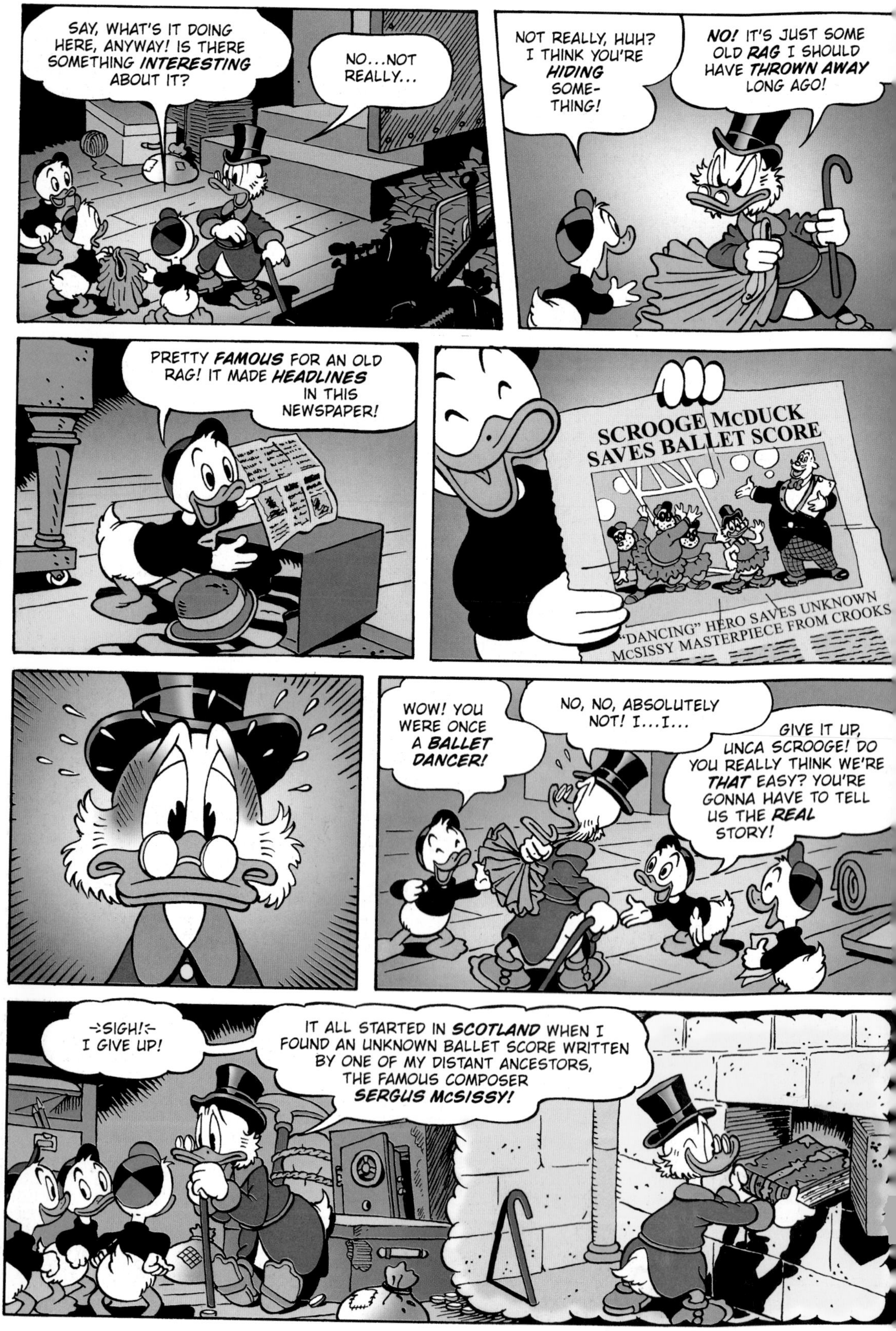

SAY, WHAT'S IT DOING HERE, ANYWAY! IS THERE SOMETHING INTERESTING ABOUT IT?
NO...NOT REALLY...
NOT REALLY, HUH? I THINK YOU'RE HIDING SOME-THING!
NO! IT'S JUST SOME OLD RAG I SHOULD HAVE THROWN AWAY LONG AGO!
PRETTY FAMOUS FOR AN OLD RAG! IT MADE HEADLINES IN THIS NEWSPAPER!
SCROOGE McDUCK SAVES BALLET SCORE
"DANCING" HERO SAVES UNKNOWN McSISSY MASTERPIECE FROM CROOKS
WOW! YOU WERE ONCE A BALLET DANCER!
NO, NO, ABSOLUTELY NOT! I...I...
GIVE IT UP, UNCA SCROOGE! DO YOU REALLY THINK WE'RE THAT EASY? YOU'RE GONNA HAVE TO TELL US THE REAL STORY!
-SIGH!- I GIVE UP!
IT ALL STARTED IN SCOTLAND WHEN I FOUND AN UNKNOWN BALLET SCORE WRITTEN BY ONE OF MY DISTANT ANCESTORS, THE FAMOUS COMPOSER SERGUS McSISSY!

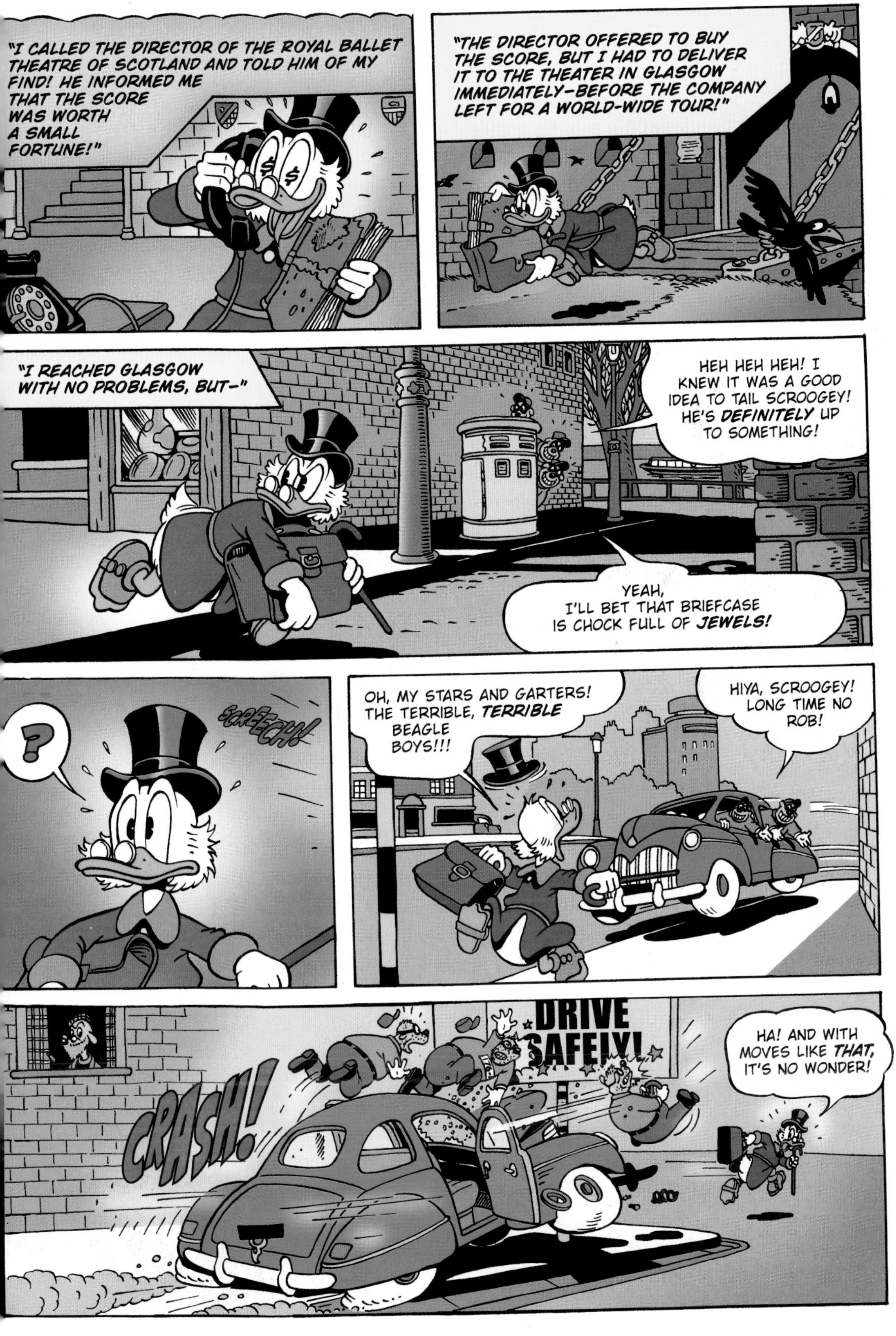
"I CALLED THE DIRECTOR OF THE ROYAL BALLET THEATRE OF SCOTLAND AND TOLD HIM OF MY FIND! HE INFORMED ME THAT THE SCORE WAS WORTH A SMALL FORTUNE!"
"THE DIRECTOR OFFERED TO BUY THE SCORE, BUT I HAD TO DELIVER IT TO THE THEATER IN GLASGOW IMMEDIATELY–BEFORE THE COMPANY LEFT FOR A WORLD-WIDE TOUR!"
"I REACHED GLASGOW WITH NO PROBLEMS, BUT–"
HEH HEH HEH! I KNEW IT WAS A GOOD IDEA TO TAIL SCROOGEY! HE'S DEFINITELY UP TO SOMETHING!
YEAH, I'LL BET THAT BRIEFCASE IS CHOCK FULL OF JEWELS!
?
SCREECH!
OH, MY STARS AND GARTERS! THE TERRIBLE, TERRIBLE BEAGLE BOYS!!!
HIYA, SCROOGEY! LONG TIME NO ROB!
CRASH!
DRIVE SAFELY!
HA! AND WITH MOVES LIKE THAT, IT'S NO WONDER!

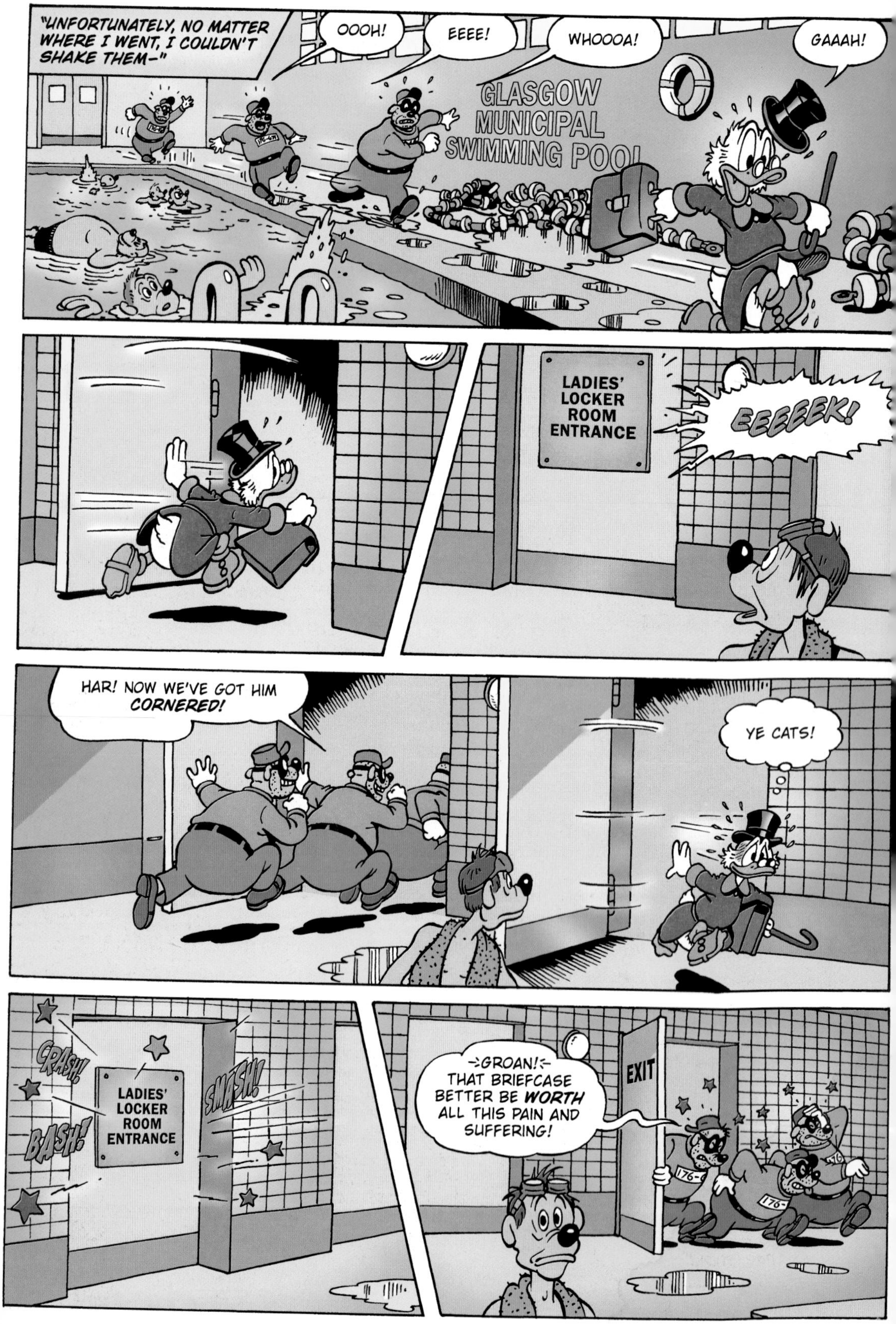
"UNFORTUNATELY, NO MATTER WHERE I WENT, I COULDN'T SHAKE THEM—"
OOOH!
EEEE!
WHOOOA!
GAAAH!
GLASGOW MUNICIPAL SWIMMING POOL
LADIES' LOCKER ROOM ENTRANCE
EEEEEK!
HAR! NOW WE'VE GOT HIM *CORNERED!*
YE CATS!
CRASH!
BASH!
SMASH!
LADIES' LOCKER ROOM ENTRANCE
EXIT
-GROAN!- THAT BRIEFCASE BETTER BE *WORTH* ALL THIS PAIN AND SUFFERING!

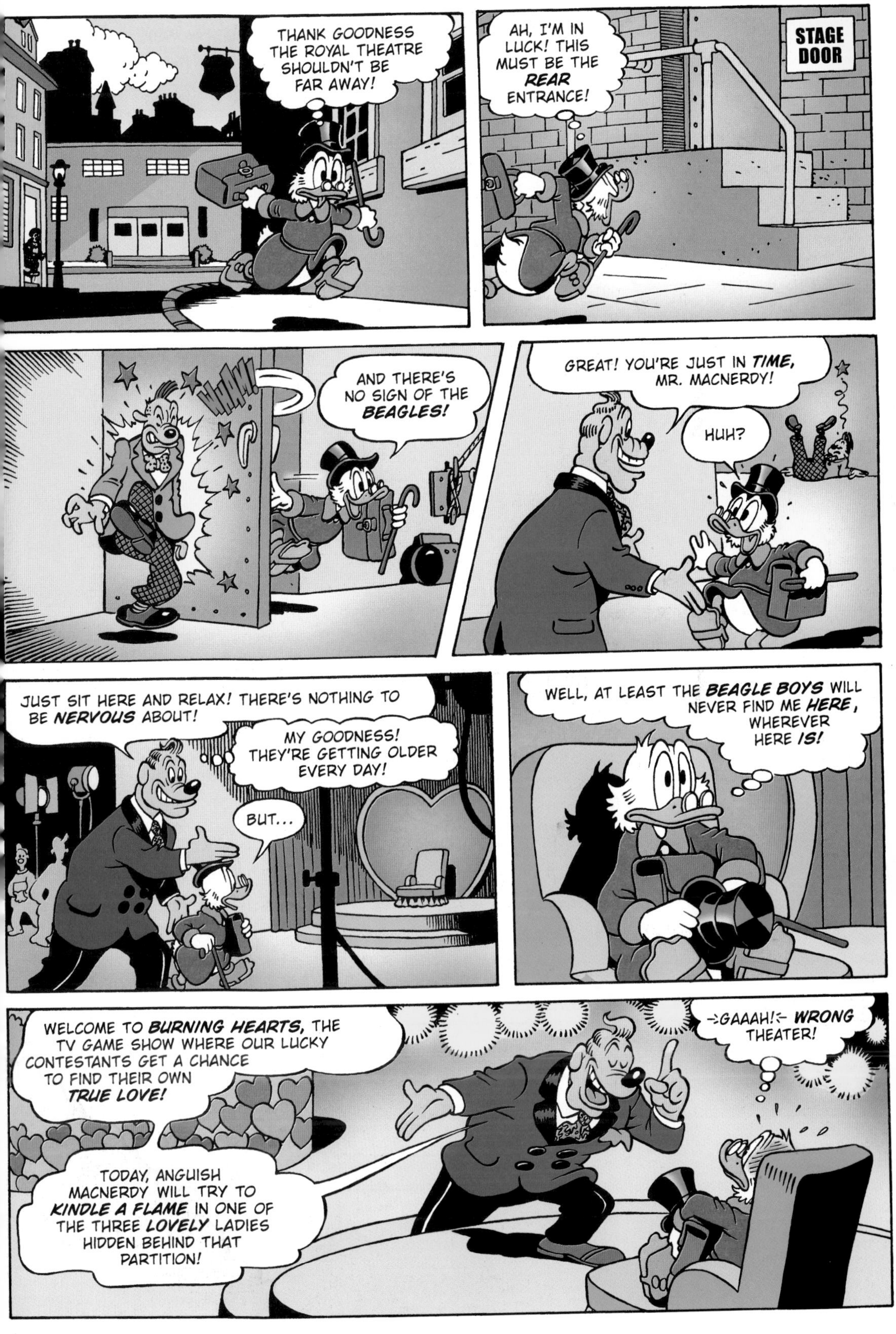
THANK GOODNESS THE ROYAL THEATRE SHOULDN'T BE FAR AWAY!
AH, I'M IN LUCK! THIS MUST BE THE **REAR** ENTRANCE!
STAGE DOOR
WHAM!
AND THERE'S NO SIGN OF THE **BEAGLES!**
GREAT! YOU'RE JUST IN **TIME,** MR. MACNERDY!
HUH?
JUST SIT HERE AND RELAX! THERE'S NOTHING TO BE **NERVOUS** ABOUT!
MY GOODNESS! THEY'RE GETTING OLDER EVERY DAY!
BUT...
WELL, AT LEAST THE **BEAGLE BOYS** WILL NEVER FIND ME **HERE,** WHEREVER HERE **IS!**
WELCOME TO **BURNING HEARTS,** THE TV GAME SHOW WHERE OUR LUCKY CONTESTANTS GET A CHANCE TO FIND THEIR OWN **TRUE LOVE!**
TODAY, ANGUISH MACNERDY WILL TRY TO **KINDLE A FLAME** IN ONE OF THE THREE **LOVELY** LADIES HIDDEN BEHIND THAT PARTITION!
→GAAAH!← **WRONG** THEATER!

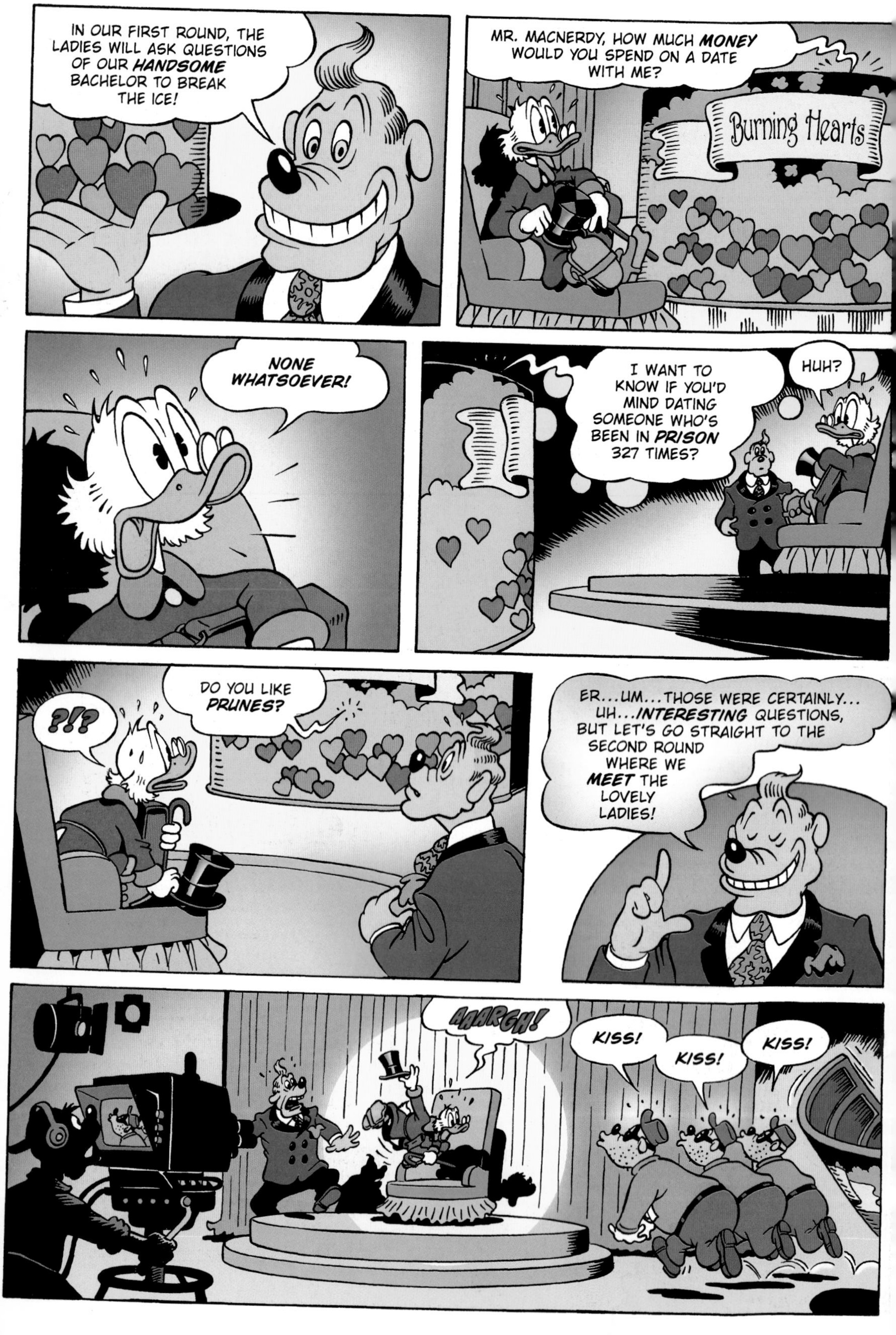
IN OUR FIRST ROUND, THE LADIES WILL ASK QUESTIONS OF OUR HANDSOME BACHELOR TO BREAK THE ICE!
MR. MACNERDY, HOW MUCH MONEY WOULD YOU SPEND ON A DATE WITH ME?
Burning Hearts
NONE WHATSOEVER!
I WANT TO KNOW IF YOU'D MIND DATING SOMEONE WHO'S BEEN IN PRISON 327 TIMES?
HUH?
?!?
DO YOU LIKE PRUNES?
ER...UM...THOSE WERE CERTAINLY... UH...INTERESTING QUESTIONS, BUT LET'S GO STRAIGHT TO THE SECOND ROUND WHERE WE MEET THE LOVELY LADIES!
AAARGH!
KISS!
KISS!
KISS!

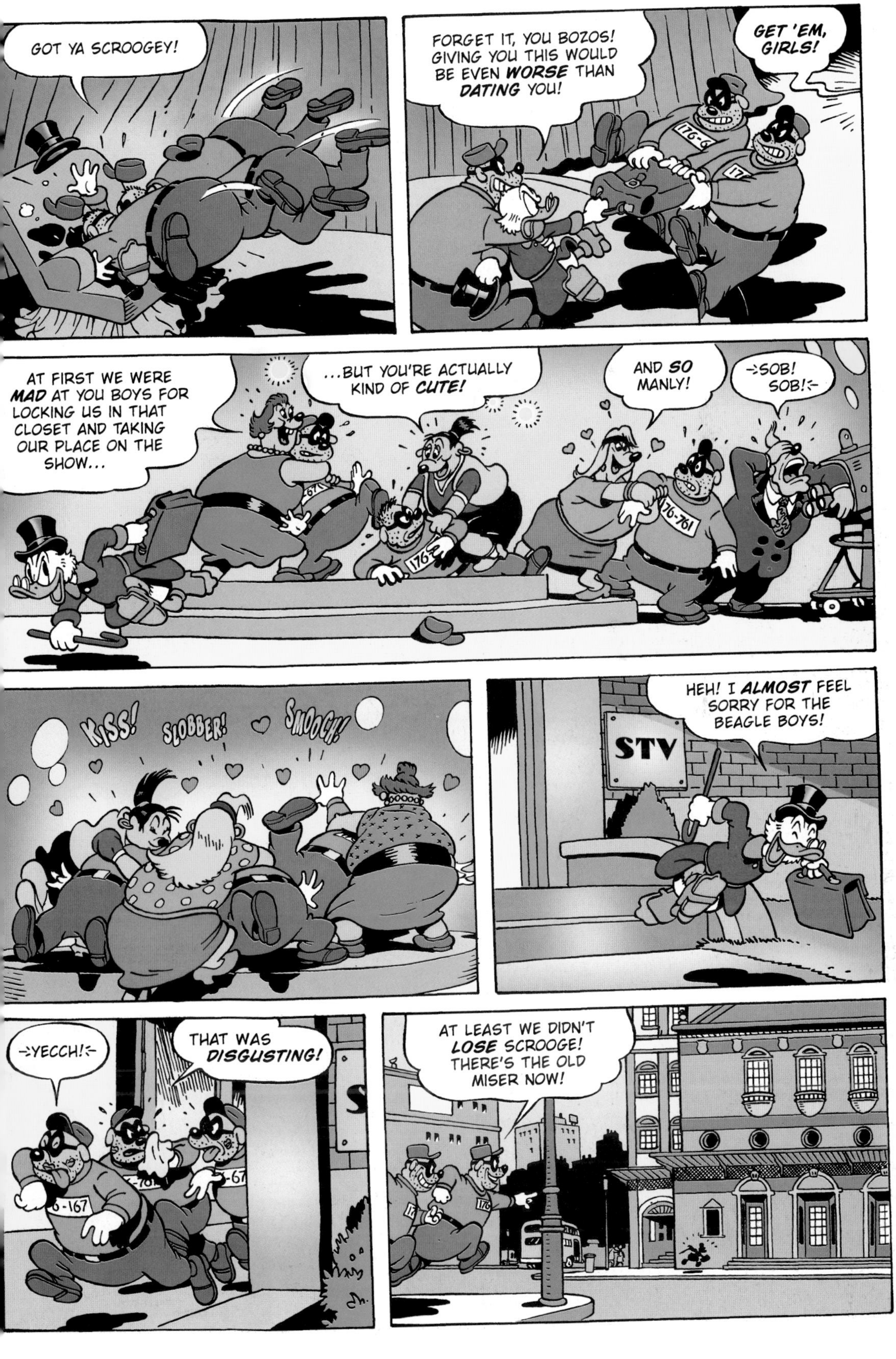
GOT YA SCROOGEY!
FORGET IT, YOU BOZOS! GIVING YOU THIS WOULD BE EVEN WORSE THAN DATING YOU!
GET 'EM, GIRLS!
AT FIRST WE WERE MAD AT YOU BOYS FOR LOCKING US IN THAT CLOSET AND TAKING OUR PLACE ON THE SHOW...
...BUT YOU'RE ACTUALLY KIND OF CUTE!
AND SO MANLY!
SOB! SOB!
KISS!
SLOBBER!
SMOOCH!
STV
HEH! I ALMOST FEEL SORRY FOR THE BEAGLE BOYS!
YECCH!
THAT WAS DISGUSTING!
AT LEAST WE DIDN'T LOSE SCROOGE! THERE'S THE OLD MISER NOW!

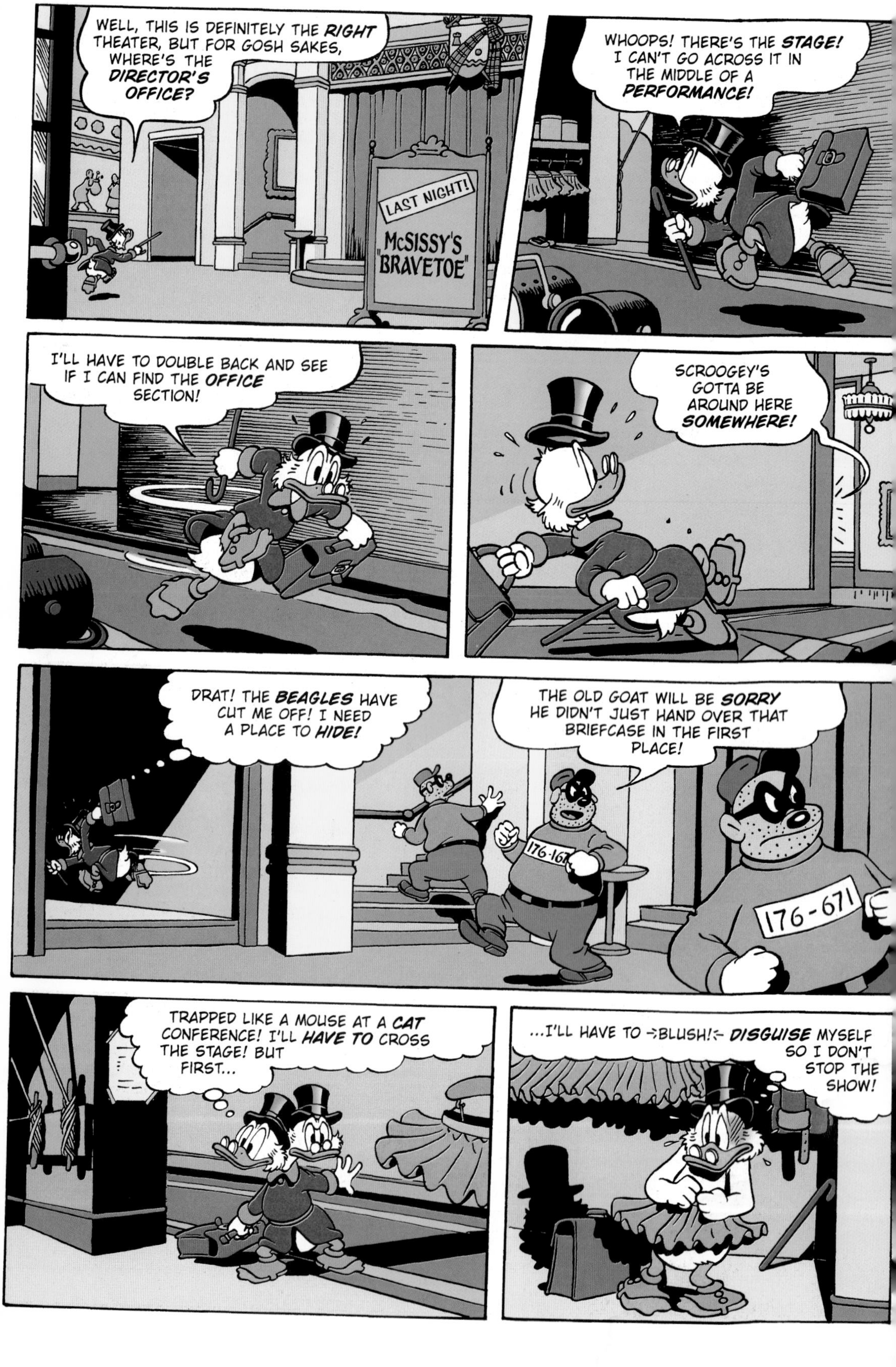
WELL, THIS IS DEFINITELY THE RIGHT THEATER, BUT FOR GOSH SAKES, WHERE'S THE DIRECTOR'S OFFICE?
LAST NIGHT!
McSISSY'S "BRAVETOE"
WHOOPS! THERE'S THE STAGE! I CAN'T GO ACROSS IT IN THE MIDDLE OF A PERFORMANCE!
I'LL HAVE TO DOUBLE BACK AND SEE IF I CAN FIND THE OFFICE SECTION!
SCROOGEY'S GOTTA BE AROUND HERE SOMEWHERE!
DRAT! THE BEAGLES HAVE CUT ME OFF! I NEED A PLACE TO HIDE!
THE OLD GOAT WILL BE SORRY HE DIDN'T JUST HAND OVER THAT BRIEFCASE IN THE FIRST PLACE!
176-167
176-671
TRAPPED LIKE A MOUSE AT A CAT CONFERENCE! I'LL HAVE TO CROSS THE STAGE! BUT FIRST...
...I'LL HAVE TO →BLUSH!← DISGUISE MYSELF SO I DON'T STOP THE SHOW!

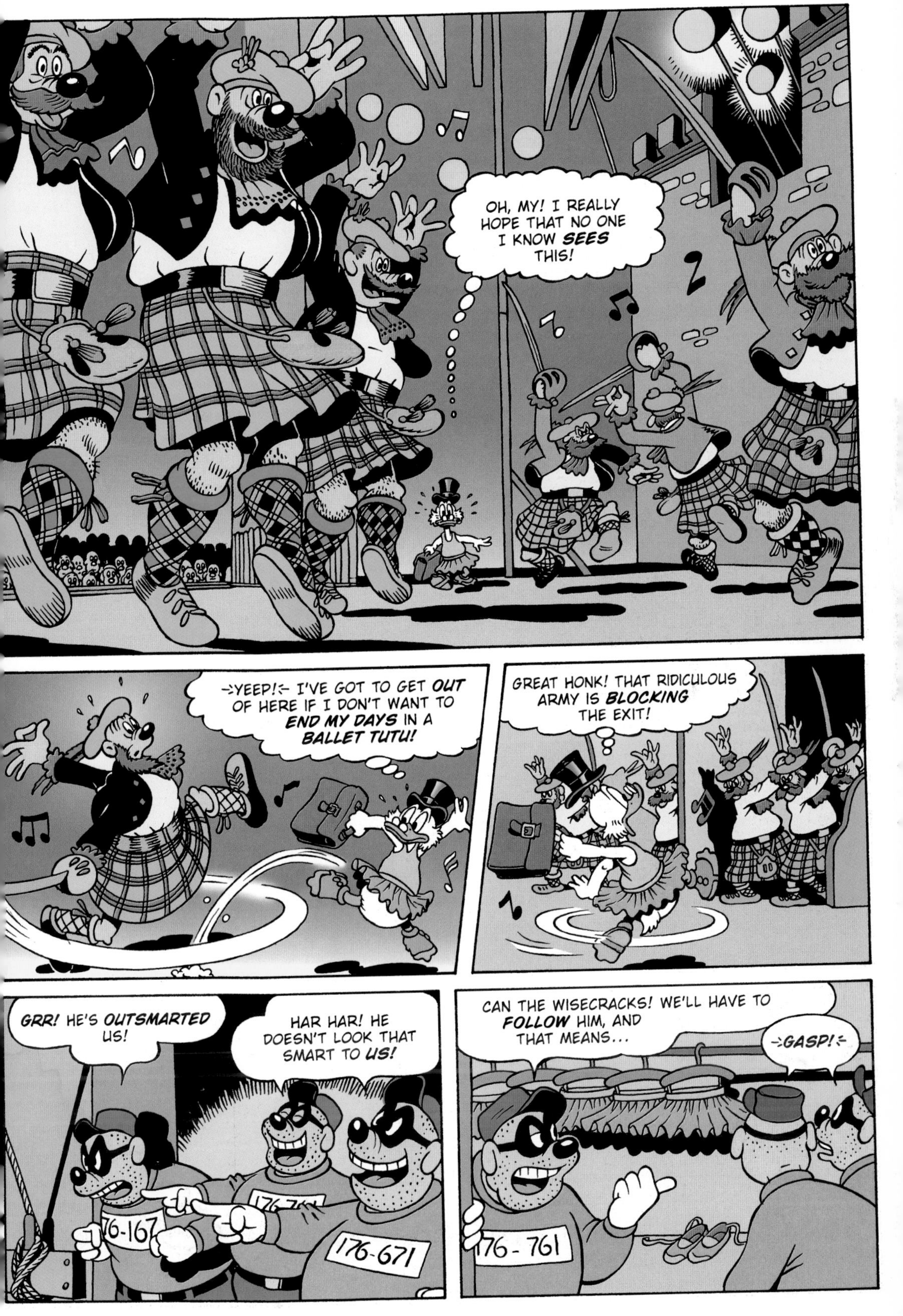
OH, MY! I REALLY HOPE THAT NO ONE I KNOW SEES THIS!
-YEEP!- I'VE GOT TO GET OUT OF HERE IF I DON'T WANT TO END MY DAYS IN A BALLET TUTU!
GREAT HONK! THAT RIDICULOUS ARMY IS BLOCKING THE EXIT!
GRR! HE'S OUTSMARTED US!
HAR HAR! HE DOESN'T LOOK THAT SMART TO US!
176-167
176-671
CAN THE WISECRACKS! WE'LL HAVE TO FOLLOW HIM, AND THAT MEANS...
-GASP!-
176-761

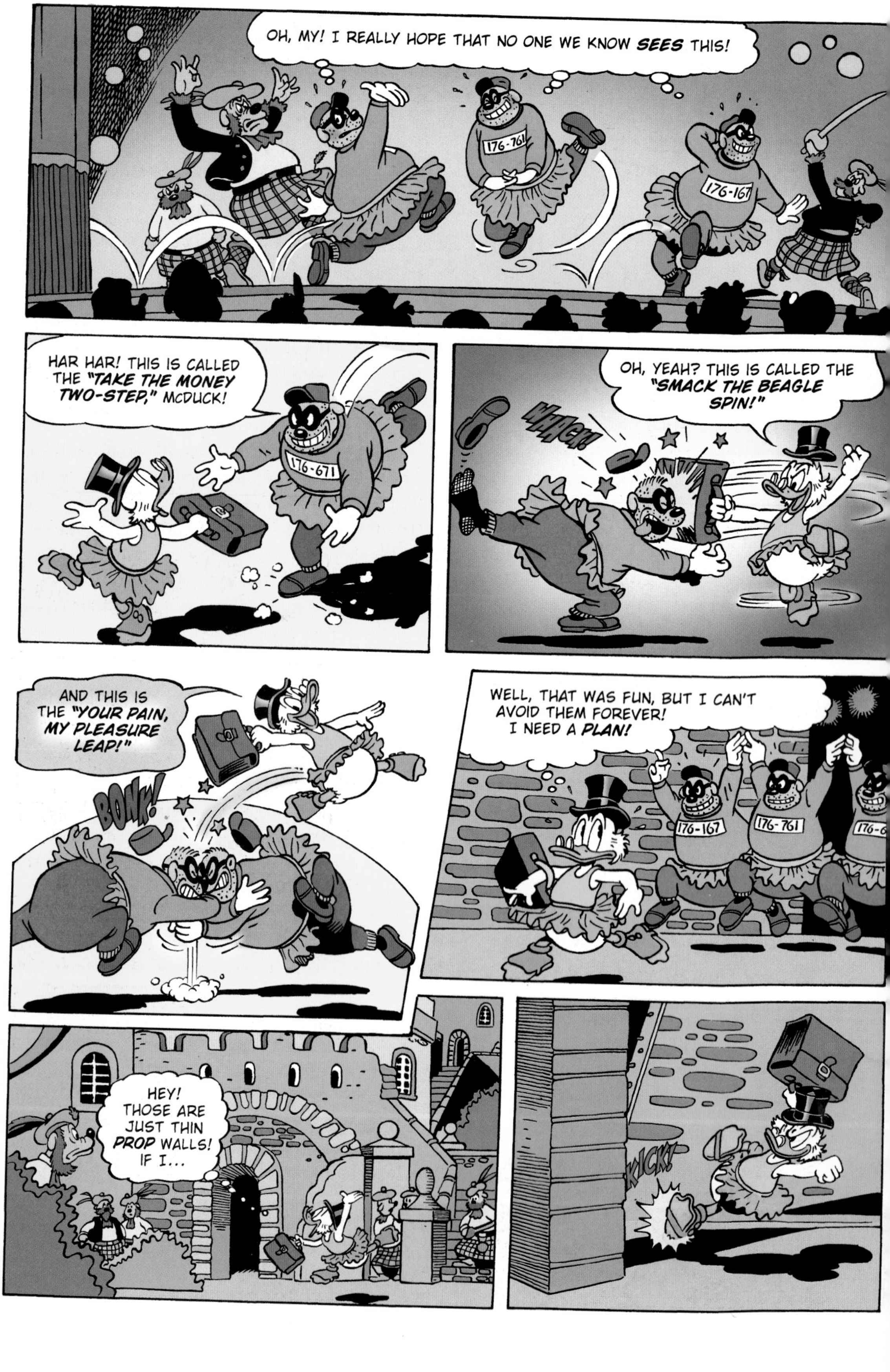
OH, MY! I REALLY HOPE THAT NO ONE WE KNOW SEES THIS!
176-761
176-167
HAR HAR! THIS IS CALLED THE "TAKE THE MONEY TWO-STEP," McDUCK!
176-671
OH, YEAH? THIS IS CALLED THE "SMACK THE BEAGLE SPIN!"
WHACK!
AND THIS IS THE "YOUR PAIN, MY PLEASURE LEAP!"
BONK!
WELL, THAT WAS FUN, BUT I CAN'T AVOID THEM FOREVER! I NEED A PLAN!
176-167
176-761
HEY! THOSE ARE JUST THIN PROP WALLS! IF I...
KICK!

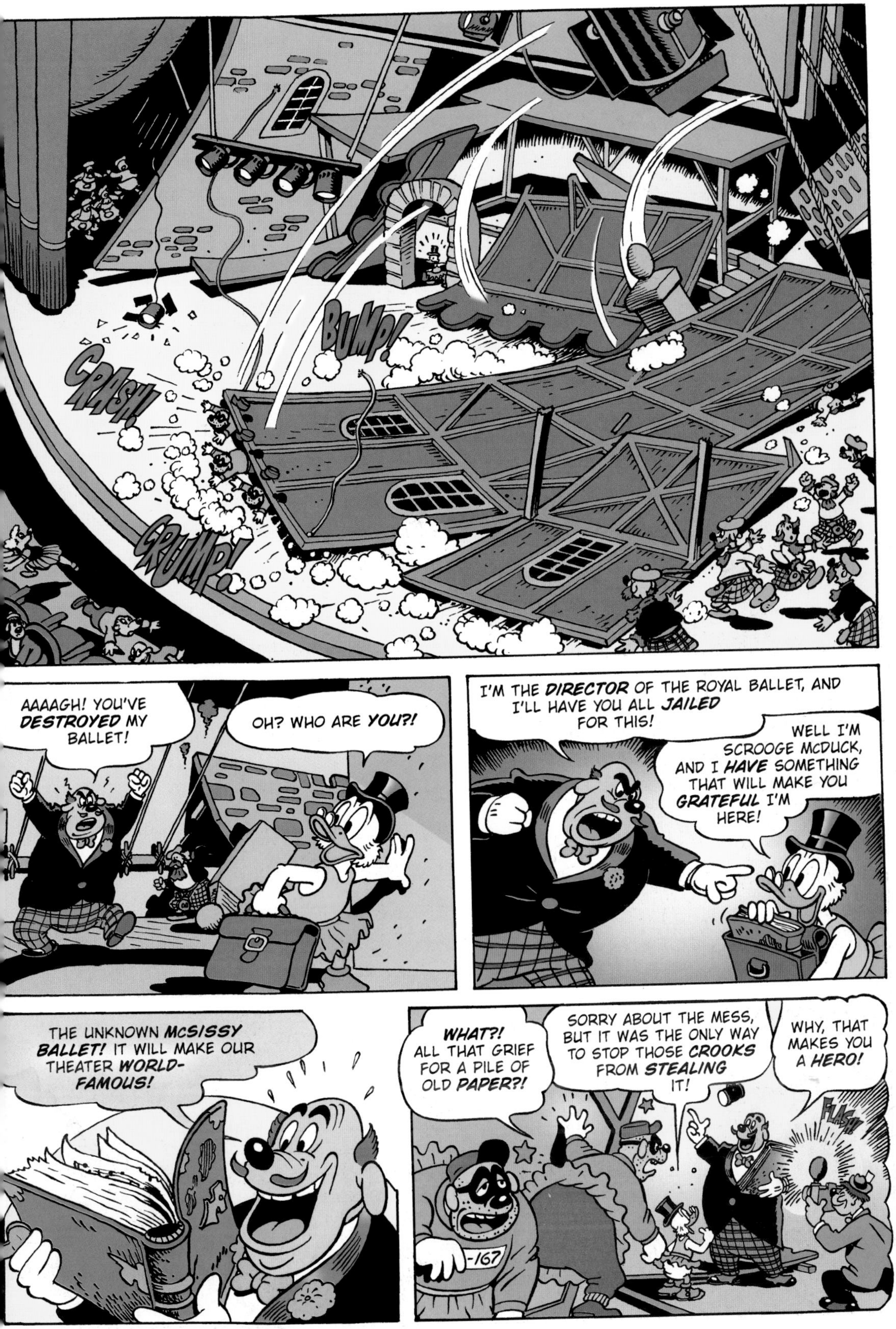

BUMP!
CRASH!
CRUMP!
AAAAGH! YOU'VE DESTROYED MY BALLET!
OH? WHO ARE YOU?!
I'M THE DIRECTOR OF THE ROYAL BALLET, AND I'LL HAVE YOU ALL JAILED FOR THIS!
WELL I'M SCROOGE McDUCK, AND I HAVE SOMETHING THAT WILL MAKE YOU GRATEFUL I'M HERE!
THE UNKNOWN McSISSY BALLET! IT WILL MAKE OUR THEATER WORLD-FAMOUS!
WHAT?! ALL THAT GRIEF FOR A PILE OF OLD PAPER?!
SORRY ABOUT THE MESS, BUT IT WAS THE ONLY WAY TO STOP THOSE CROOKS FROM STEALING IT!
WHY, THAT MAKES YOU A HERO!
FLASH!
-167

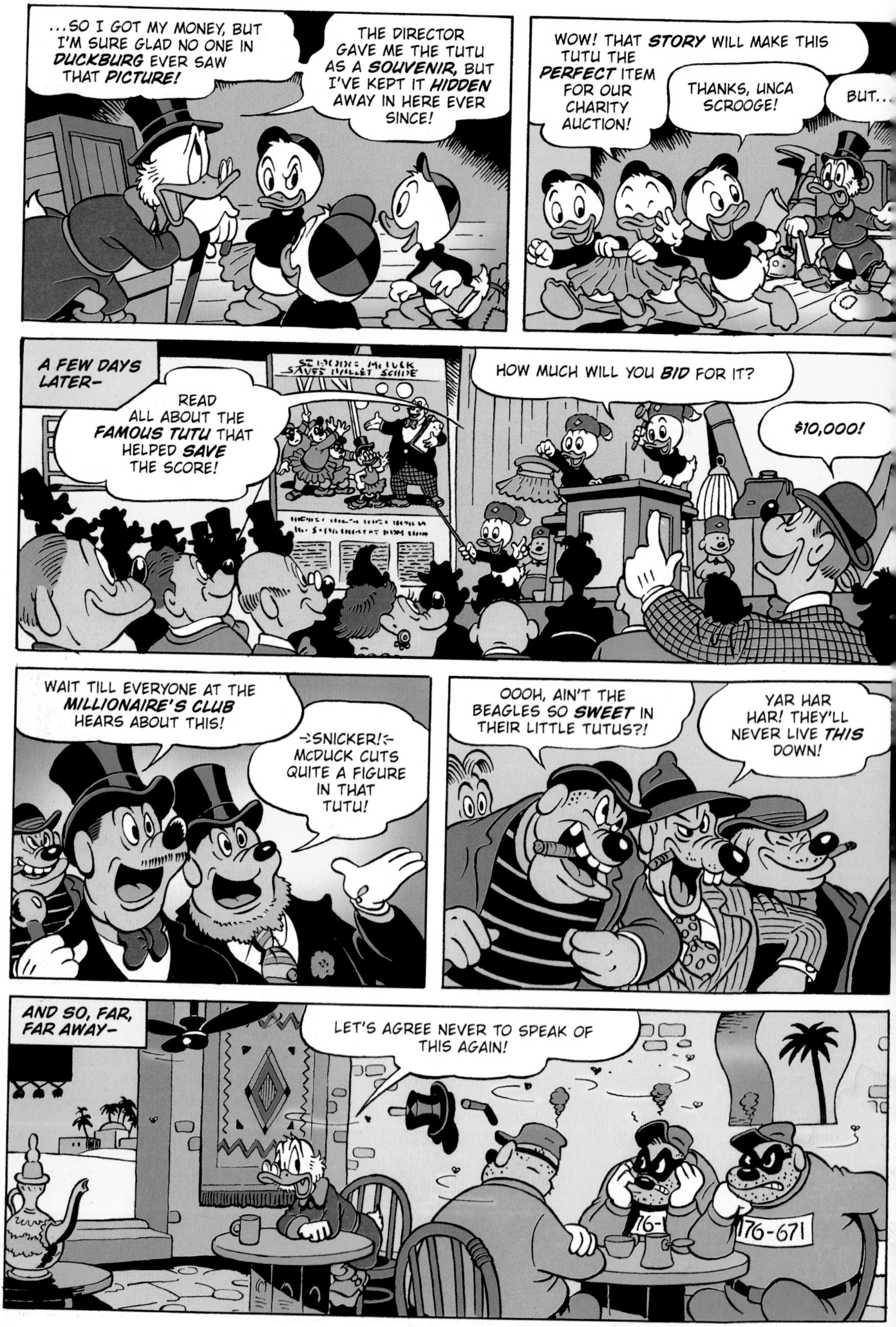
...SO I GOT MY MONEY, BUT I'M SURE GLAD NO ONE IN DUCKBURG EVER SAW THAT PICTURE!
THE DIRECTOR GAVE ME THE TUTU AS A SOUVENIR, BUT I'VE KEPT IT HIDDEN AWAY IN HERE EVER SINCE!
WOW! THAT STORY WILL MAKE THIS TUTU THE PERFECT ITEM FOR OUR CHARITY AUCTION!
THANKS, UNCA SCROOGE!
BUT...
A FEW DAYS LATER-
READ ALL ABOUT THE FAMOUS TUTU THAT HELPED SAVE THE SCORE!
HOW MUCH WILL YOU BID FOR IT?
$10,000!
WAIT TILL EVERYONE AT THE MILLIONAIRE'S CLUB HEARS ABOUT THIS!
-SNICKER!- McDUCK CUTS QUITE A FIGURE IN THAT TUTU!
OOOH, AIN'T THE BEAGLES SO SWEET IN THEIR LITTLE TUTUS?!
YAR HAR HAR! THEY'LL NEVER LIVE THIS DOWN!
AND SO, FAR, FAR AWAY-
LET'S AGREE NEVER TO SPEAK OF THIS AGAIN!
76-
176-671

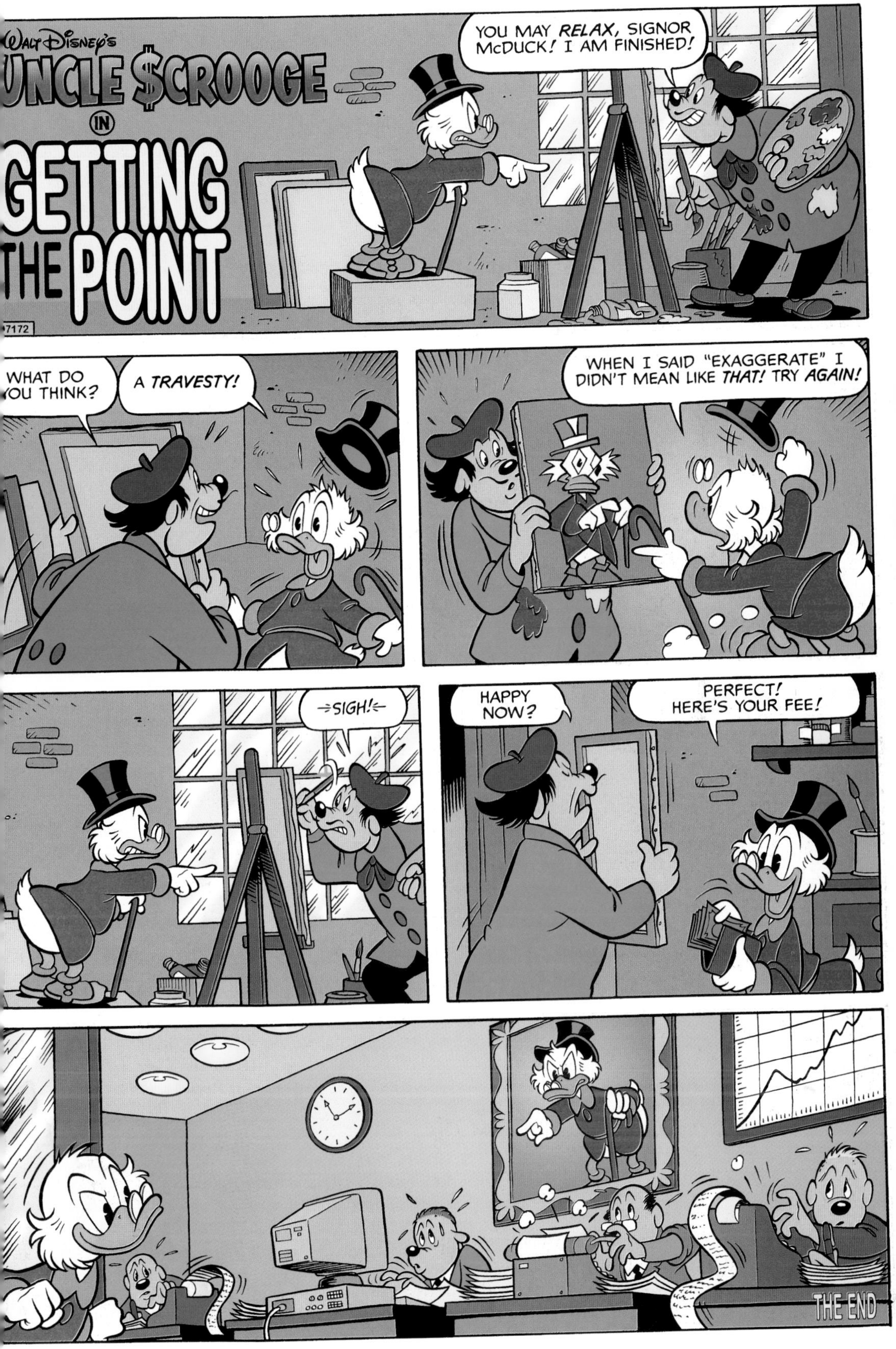
WALT DISNEY'S
UNCLE $CROOGE
IN
GETTING THE POINT
7172
YOU MAY RELAX, SIGNOR McDUCK! I AM FINISHED!
WHAT DO YOU THINK?
A TRAVESTY!
WHEN I SAID "EXAGGERATE" I DIDN'T MEAN LIKE THAT! TRY AGAIN!
SIGH!
HAPPY NOW?
PERFECT! HERE'S YOUR FEE!
THE END